DEEP TROUBLE

According to his file Rob Stevens lives on the Dorset coast with his wife and two young sons. He grew up in Bournemouth before studying Engineering at Cambridge University – a notorious MI6 recruiting ground. Government documents list his occupation as 'Airline Pilot', which would be the perfect cover for, say, a spy undertaking frequent foreign assignments. MI6 denies that he is a Secret Agent – which is exactly what you would expect them to say.

S.T.I.N.K. B.O.M.B.*

DEEP TROUBLE

***Secret Team of Intrepid-Natured Kids
Battling Odious Masterminds (Basically)**

ROB STEVENS

Printed and bound by CPI Group (UK) Ltd, Croydon CR0 4YY

MACMILLAN CHILDREN'S BOOKS

First published 2012 by Macmillan Children's Books
a division of Macmillan Publishers Limited
20 New Wharf Road, London N1 9RR
Basingstoke and Oxford
Associated companies throughout the world
www.panmacmillan.com

ISBN 978-0-330-53026-2

1 3 5 7 9 8 6 4 2

A CIP catalogue record for this book is available from
the British Library.

For Anna, Sophie, Helena and Issy

I'd like to thank everyone at Macmillan Children's Books for their hard work – especially Emma Young and Samantha Swinnerton. I am grateful to my agent, Madeleine Buston, for her advice, and to all my friends and family who take such a close interest in my literary endeavours. Most of all I want to thank three very special agents, who make every mission a joy – my wife Clare and my two sons, Dylan and Charlie.

At a Secret Location – Somewhere Near London . . .

Chapter 1

The female assassin pointed the gun between the man's eyes. Or rather, between his eye and the puckered scar where his other eye used to be.

'When I pull this trigger,' she said calmly, 'you will be unrecognisable, even to your own brother.'

The man's Adam's apple bobbed in his scrawny throat. 'I don't want to die,' he snivelled, a slimy yellow worm slithering out of the hole in his face where his nose should have been.

'Oh, don't be so melodramatic, Kurt,' said the woman, rolling her piercing green eyes. 'It's hardly as if your life is worth anything – you're so *ugly*.'

She placed her left hand over the gun's bulbous capsule-shaped chamber and cocked it.

'But . . .'

'It's no good. I simply can't *bear* to look at your hideous face any more.'

'No!' Kurt protested.

Closing one eye, the assassin aimed the gun and squeezed the trigger.

'Aaaarghh!' Kurt screamed as a cone of fine mist sprayed gently over his face.

'Oh, don't be such a baby!' the woman rebuked. 'And do keep still, there's a good boy.'

Realising that the liquid coating his skin was actually painless, Kurt stopped screaming. The fluid dried instantly on contact, turning into a thin rubbery mask. The gun automatically controlled the distribution of the spray, building layer on layer, like the contours of a map, to create brand-new features.

When the spraying stopped, Kurt had been transformed. He had slightly sagging jowls, a hooked nose and large ears with fleshy lobes. His single eye blinked from behind his lifelike latex mask. The woman jabbed her thumb and forefinger into the mask's empty eye socket, stretched the lids apart, and popped in a glass eyeball.

'There,' she said, handing him a mirror. 'Something

of an improvement, I'm sure you'll agree.'

Kurt admired himself, grinning at the brand-new features looking back at him. 'I'm handsome,' he announced proudly.

'Let's not get carried away, darling,' the woman sneered. 'I think *normal* is about the best we can say. But that's good. When you're working undercover the last thing you want is to stand out from the crowd, which is why my beauty has been *such* a curse.' Snatching the mirror back, she tilted her head and teased a couple of tresses of her long flame-red hair.

'Whose face have you given me?' Kurt asked, feeling the end of his freshly applied prosthetic nose.

'Nobody special,' the assassin replied, absently stroking her thick eyelashes with the back of one finger. 'I utilised the randomiser function on the Face-mapping-quick-drying-liquid-latex-mask-gun. It has thousands of facial maps stored in its database so I just told it I wanted a middle-aged man. I could just as easily have turned you into a schoolgirl or an old woman.'

A second man, who had been watching the demonstration with interest, started to chuckle. He was muscular with a shaved head and a single continuous eyebrow growing along the ridge of his low forehead.

'He's always been a bit of an old woman,' muttered Klaus Von Grosskopf – Kurt's brother.

'No I'm not – you are,' Kurt whined.

'You are.'

'You are.'

'Am not.'

'Are so.'

'Silence!' the woman snarled. 'We don't have time for your petty bickering. We have to plan carefully if we're going to get our target without being noticed. Fortunately, thanks to the Face-mapping-quick-drying-liquid-latex-mask-gun, the perfect disguise is literally at our fingertips.'

'Who is the target?' asked Kurt.

'Him.' The woman thrust a photograph into Kurt's hands. 'And it's going to be all the more enjoyable taking him out in front of hundreds of people.'

Chapter 2

'Red Alert!' Barney Jones grimaced. 'I repeat, Red Alert.'

'Are you sure it's that serious?' Archie whispered.

'That's a roger. This is a Priority One.' Barney's head swivelled from side to side. 'There's nothing here. I'll try the adjacent premises. If I'm not back in five . . .'

'I'll wait,' Archie said, pushing his glasses up his nose. 'I'm not leaving without you.'

Barney nodded, then turned to leave. 'All units, we have a go,' he muttered, holding his wrist to his chin, as though talking into a cuff mic. 'Operation Emergency Chocolate Bar is live.'

Archie watched Barney's stocky figure leave the bookshop. It had been an hour since they'd had a milkshake and a cookie in Starbucks so he wasn't surprised that his best friend was in desperate need of another sugar fix. While he waited for Barney to return from the sweet shop next door he browsed the magazines on the shelves.

Almost ten minutes later Archie looked up from a copy of *National Geographic Kids* and glanced over his shoulder to see what was taking Barney so long. Instantly his mouth dried up and his pulse thrummed. The man standing about ten metres away was middle-aged, with short dark hair and a wispy moustache. He was wearing a green cagoule, brown cords and brogues. He didn't appear to be a particularly threatening character, but Archie had noticed him loitering nearby in the last three shops they'd been in, which could only mean one thing.

They were being followed.

Turning away from the man in the green cagoule, Archie lowered his head, as if reading his magazine, and tried to think up a plan.

Six months had passed since MI6 had recruited Archie and Barney to join its brand-new sub-agency employing a team of uniquely talented kids as spies. The team had been named S.T.I.N.K.B.O.M.B. which stood for Secret Team of Intrepid-Natured Kids Battling

8

Odious Masterminds, Basically.

MI6 Team Leader, Helen Highwater, had been joking when she had suggested using kids for surveillance operations because teenagers were better qualified than anyone to sit around all day doing nothing. But the Director General had loved her idea and appointed her Initiative Commander (IC) of the fledgling team.

When Highwater found herself facing a potential EMU (Evil Mastermind Uprising) most of her existing agents were unavailable for duty. Agent Kilo was grounded, Agent Alpha had chickenpox and Agent Uniform had just had her tonsils out. With Agent Hotel nursing a broken ankle, sustained playing football in the school playground, the only existing agent available to track down the enigmatic Dr Doom had been skilled computer hacker, fourteen-year-old Gemma Croft, aka Agent X-ray.

Determined to recruit someone to accompany Agent X-ray on this assignment, Highwater had consulted SPADE – MI6's Secret Potential Agent Data Evaluator. SPADE had identified twelve-year-old Archie Hunt as an ideal candidate because of his intelligence, linguistic ability and aptitude for problem-solving. He also happened to be a skilled pilot (taught by his father who was an ex-Special Forces pilot and millionaire businessman), as well as being genetically predisposed to excel at martial arts. His mother, who died when he was nine, had herself been an MI6 operative and an expert in hand-to-hand combat.

Barney Jones boasted none of Archie's natural aptitude for being a secret agent and his SPADE score had been pretty average. But he was fanatical about spy films and books and he had managed to talk his way on to the team with his encyclopedic knowledge of Evil Masterminds.

Archie had been given the codename Agent Yankee and Barney became Agent Zulu. Together with Agent X-ray the three kids had embarked on STINKBOMB's first mission, to thwart Dr Doom (aka Yuri Villenemi) in his quest to create the ultimate super-being and take over the world.

The assignment had been so successful that MI6 had designated Archie, Barney and Gemma to Team Alpha, while the other four agents had been assigned to Team Bravo.

All STINKBOMB agents had been taught that if their cover was compromised they could be valuable assets to terrorists, as well as a target for any Evil Mastermind with a grudge against the British government. Whether the stalker was an assassin or a kidnapper or just an innocent shopper, Archie knew he had to give him the slip and head for the nearest safe house.

'Mission accomplished.' Barney slung a friendly arm around Archie's shoulder. 'Sorry that took so long,' he said, his voice distorted by a mouthful of chocolate. 'I couldn't decide whether to get a Twix or a Picnic.'

'So you got them both?' said Archie, nodding at Barney's handful of confectionery. 'Plus some crisps and a bag of Liquorice Allsorts?'

'As a precaution.' Barney's plump cheeks squeezed into a grin. 'Just in case. Anyway, how come you're looking so shifty?'

'Don't look now,' Archie muttered through the corner of his mouth. 'But I think we've got a tail.' Raising a hand to scratch his mass of mousy brown hair, Archie jerked his head towards the stalker.

'Where?' Barney yelped, snapping on to tiptoes and peering over the magazine racks like a prairie dog scanning for predators.

Archie yanked Barney back down and whispered sharply, 'Keep your voice down! The last thing we need is for him to know we've clocked him. Just act natural.'

11

'Copy that.' Barney dropped into a low crouch. Parting some copies of *Hello!* on the bottom shelf he peered through the gap towards the checkout.

'If I tell you who the mark is, do you *promise* to be subtle?' asked Archie.

Barney nodded slowly, apparently unaware that the magazine he was earnestly pretending to study was the latest edition of *Just Seventeen*.

Archie's heart was hammering against his ribcage but he told himself to relax. If he panicked he might make irrational decisions that could lead to fatal mistakes. 'In my four o'clock,' he said calmly. 'Ten metres away. Cagoule, sensible shoes, 'tache.'

Barney peeked over the top of the magazine and twisted robotically at the waist. 'Contact,' he said definitively. 'Although I think it's unfair to say she's got a moustache. Quite a lot of older ladies – like my nan for instance – get a few whiskers but I wouldn't class that as—'

'Not *her*,' Archie interrupted. He was pretending to study his iPhone while actually using a mirror app to look over his shoulder. 'The man next to her. I've noticed him in the last three shops we've been in. And now he's over there reading *Model Railways Monthly*.

12

Doesn't that strike you as weird?'

'Well weird,' Barney agreed. 'I mean, what kind of grown-up spends his spare time playing with toy trains?'

'Not the magazine, you wally. I mean it's weird that he seems to show up everywhere we go.'

'Good point. What's the plan?'

'I say we leave now,' Archie said. 'You'll have to finish reading about "Ten Bikinis for Winter Sun" another time.'

Realising what he'd been pretending to read, Barney blushed, slipped it behind a copy of *Shoot!* and followed Archie outside. 'We are on the move,' Barney muttered. 'I say again, the mongoose is migrating.'

Forcing himself to walk at a steady pace, Archie exited the shop and turned left. Barney was swinging his arms frenetically as he struggled to catch up without breaking into a telltale run.

It had been raining since mid-morning but the street was still rammed with weekend shoppers, heads bowed against the icy winter air. The two boys tried to weave through the crowd without causing any commotion. Archie knew they were safer among lots of people but he felt uncomfortable not knowing how close the man in the green cagoule was. He paused, pretending to look in a shop window and stole a quick glance over his shoulder. The man was just a few metres behind them.

'What do you think he wants?' Barney wheezed.

Archie pushed his rectangular glasses up his nose and scratched his head through his tangle of brown hair. 'No idea. But if we don't do something quick he'll have us right where he wants us.'

Three more shops remained on the High Street, but beyond that lay the dangerous desertion of common land.

'How about splitting up?' suggested Barney.

Archie shook his head. 'It's safer if we stay together. At least we stand a fighting chance if he corners us.' In truth Archie was quietly confident of defending himself, having recently discovered a natural flair for martial arts during STINKBOMB's first mission. But he knew Barney might not fare as well on his own.

Desperately scanning the mass of shoppers, Archie saw their chance. Coming the other way, wearing assorted anoraks and matching rucksacks, was a long line of foreign-language-school children. With each child holding on to the backpack of the child in front, the school party formed a continuous line that was making tortuously slow progress. Stationed around the human crocodile were eight adults, presumably teachers, chaperoning the children, like bodyguards around a presidential cortège.

Archie knew they would have to time their move perfectly. He waited until the children were just about to pass in front of the entrance to a big department store.

'In here. Quick!'

Suddenly Archie grabbed Barney's wrist and hauled him sideways. The two boys darted across the flow of human traffic, brushing in front of the teacher at the head of the school party.

'Sorry, miss!' Barney called over his shoulder.

As they jogged into the shop Archie spun round to check on their pursuer and saw the man in the green cagoule still outside. His head and shoulders were visible beyond the procession of schoolkids who were blocking his path to the doorway. He was frowning and frantically scanning the line of children. Suddenly he looked up and locked his eyes on the entrance to the department store.

Archie turned and considered his options. He had to think fast.

'This way,' he whispered as he led Barney towards

the rails of women's nightwear at the back of the shop. 'I've got a plan.'

The man in the green cagoule smiled stiffly at the school kids dawdling across his path. He was tempted to barge through them but that would draw unwanted attention to him. 'Patience, old boy,' he whispered to himself. 'Assassins are invisible, like falling snow.'

Finally the line of children dispersed and he strode briskly into the shop. The delay had cost him valuable seconds, maybe a minute, and now his prey was nowhere to be seen.

He paused and searched the vast sprawl of clothes and shoppers before him, his eyes darting around eagerly. The boys might have given him the slip but they had nowhere to go. All the shop's emergency exits would be alarmed so the only way his targets could escape surreptitiously was by going out the way they came in. And to do that, they had to get past him.

The man slowly turned his head and his eyes locked on something at the far end of the store. Protruding just an inch above a clothes rail laden with women's pyjamas, he could make out a sliver of navy fabric. It was the hood of a boy's sweatshirt.

'Bingo,' he whispered.

As his eyes grew accustomed to the collage of shapes and patterns, he was able to distinguish the light grey of the other boy's hoody.

'Looks like I get to kill two birds with one stone,' he muttered. Then he strode down an aisle that led across the front of the store – initially heading ninety degrees away from his target.

Having negotiated a circuitous route round the edge of the shop, the man in the green cagoule approached the two hooded figures from behind.

'Dear oh dear,' he smiled to himself. 'This is almost too easy.'

As he came within striking range he pulled his leather gloves tight, flexing his fingers. Silently coming to a stop right behind the boys, he allowed himself a triumphant smirk.

'Bang, bang,' he mouthed. 'You're dead.'

Chapter 3

The man reached a leather-clad hand out towards the nearest boy and snatched at his collar. But, as he grabbed a fistful of material, the boy rocked forward, leaving behind his sweatshirt, which had been draped over his shoulders. With the hoody hanging limply in the man's fist the boy toppled over, like a falling tree, and hit the ground with a thwack. He lay face down, motionless – one arm twisted at an impossible angle.

Yanking the hood off the other boy's head, the man grimaced.

'I don't believe it,' he sighed. 'Outsmarted by a couple of dummies.'

*

Already a mile away, Archie and Barney were pumping the pedals on their bikes as hard as they could, steam piping through the holes in their helmets. Having disguised the mannequins in their sweatshirts, they had watched their stalker approach before heading straight for the exit. Now, dressed in soaking T-shirts and jeans, their cheeks were bright pink and their arms blotched by the wintry air.

'Nearly there,' said Archie, sensing Barney was slowing down.

'Copy that,' Barney wheezed, his tight blond curls glistening with sweat under his helmet. 'I think Operation Blind Mice has been successful, don't you?'

'Operation Blind Mice?'

'Yeah.' Barney heaved a couple more breaths. 'That's what they call losing your tail – Operation Blind Mice. Because the farmer's wife cut—'

'Yeah, I get it,' said Archie. 'I just don't remember that from any of our training exercises. Are you sure you didn't just make it up?'

'Negative.' Barney sounded offended. 'Check your manual, Agent Yankee.'

'Anyway, I think we gave him the slip,' Archie said, glancing over his shoulder. 'He's probably still looking

19

for us in the clothes department. Unless he's decided to *jacket* in.'

'I'd have thought he'd want to *hanger* round for a while,' Barney puffed. 'He probably thought he had us hemmed in.'

'Soon he'll realise he's been short-changed though,' Archie added. 'And his boss is *gown* to be really shirty.'

The boys swung into Stour Gardens and skidded to a stop outside number sixteen. After parking their bikes out of sight behind a side gate they went to the front door and rang the bell.

A teenage girl with black hair cut into a slanted fringe opened the door a couple of inches, keeping the security chain on, and peered out. She was wearing skinny black jeans and a black T-shirt.

'Girls go to college to get more knowledge,' she said evenly.

'Come on, X-ray, you know it's us,' Archie implored. 'Just let us in.'

The girl held his stare for a moment, then repeated, 'Girls go to college to get more knowledge.'

Archie and Barney exchanged a brief glance. Archie sighed and flatly recited the accepted response: 'Boys go to Jupiter to get more stupider.'

20

The girl smiled briefly, the caramel flecks in her blue eyes shining for an instant. The door closed momentarily, then it opened wide and she ushered them inside, quickly shutting and locking it behind them.

She looked the drenched boys up and down, then, with mock concern, she asked, 'Is it a bit wet outside?'

'Isn't it about time we got a new passcode?' asked Barney.

The girl shrugged. 'I quite like this one. It's so . . . true.'

'Come on, Gemma,' Archie pleaded. 'It's not fair that you get to choose all our passcodes.'

'Of course it's fair.' She folded her arms. 'I joined the agency four months before you two drips, so *technically* I am the senior agent here. Plus I'm two years older. What are you doing here anyway? You're not due any new training until next weekend.'

'We missed you, Agent X-ray, didn't we, Agent Yankee?' Barney nudged Archie as Gemma rolled her eyes.

'Very funny,' Archie sneered, trying desperately not to blush.

Helen Highwater appeared at the far end of the narrow hallway. With her blunt bobbed hair, tailored grey suit and grey silk blouse she exuded authority.

'Well why *are* you here then?' she demanded. She approached the boys and peered at them through the slender lenses of her glasses. 'This is a government safe house, not a youth club.'

'We picked up a tail,' replied Archie. Then, hoping to impress both females, he added, 'As soon as we'd identified the suspect's behaviour we successfully invoked an Operation Blind Mice.'

A loud snort of amusement escaped Gemma's mouth before she clamped her hand over it. 'More like an Operation Drowned Rat,' she muttered.

Highwater removed her spectacles and fixed Archie with her flinty eyes. 'You invoked an Operation *what*?'

Suspecting his confidence in Barney had been misplaced Archie adjusted his spectacles nervously. 'Erm . . . we invoked an Operation, uh . . . Blind Mice?'

'It means we lost our tail,' Barney added helpfully. 'Just like the three blind mi—'

'Thank you Agent Zulu,' Highwater snapped. 'I had guessed what the term referred to but it is *not* official MI6 terminology. I think we'd better go downstairs to the Ops Room for a full debrief, don't you?'

'Yes, IC,' the boys mumbled as one.

Helen Highwater led the way to the end of the corridor and down a flight of stairs into the basement. Gemma tagged on behind her and the two boys brought up the rear.

'Pssst,' Archie whispered to Barney. 'I think an apology is in order, don't you?'

Barney glanced at him and grinned. 'Don't sweat it – you weren't to know.'

'Sorry?'

'You didn't know that you were divulging classified data.' Cupping a hand over his mouth, Barney mumbled earnestly, 'Highwater's security clearance level obviously doesn't give her access to certain operational protocols. Blind Mice ops must be above her pay grade.'

Archie realised his mouth was hanging slightly open. 'And yet you are in the know?'

Barney shrugged enigmatically.

Archie let out a short laugh. 'Sometimes you are unbelievable.'

Barney accepted the comment with a modest shrug. 'Just doing my job.'

Chapter 4

The Operations Room in the basement of the Stour Gardens safe house was fortified by steel plates embedded within its ceiling and external walls. The only point of entry – the door at the foot of the stairs – looked like a typical domestic door but was actually constructed of solid steel with a wood-look veneer on the outside.

The room was dimly lit with tiny LED spotlights that created a low glow around the workstations. One wall was covered in rows of flat-screen monitors and beneath them was a long marble counter covered with numerous keyboards and laptops. The far end of the room was devoted to some sort of workshop, with soldering irons and blowtorches hanging from racks on the wall and a bench piled high with countless mechanical components.

At the other end of the basement stood a large chrome desk with a smoked glass surface, behind which sat Helen Highwater in a black leather chair. Archie, Barney and Gemma stood side by side in front of the desk.

'OK,' Highwater announced. 'Tell me – with minimal use of made-up jargon – what happened.'

While Archie described the sequence of events preceding their arrival at the safe house, Highwater listened intently, tapping a silver pen on her teeth and occasionally using it to write notes.

'Can you describe the appearance of the man who was following you?' she enquired.

'That's affirmative,' replied Barney.

'A simple yes or no would suffice,' Highwater sighed.

'Yes, that's affirmative.' Barney cleared his throat. 'He was a male ... er ... in fact he was a man ... who was wearing ... some sort of ... coat.' Barney screwed his face up and studied the ceiling.

'Agent Yankee?' asked Highwater after a lengthy silence. 'Do you have any more to add to Agent Zulu's incredibly insightful account of a male man in a coat?'

'I'd say he was six foot and pretty skinny – about a hundred and forty pounds,' Archie stated. 'He was wearing a green cagoule, brown cords and brogues. His hair was short and dark and he had a straggly moustache although he might have been wearing a disguise.'

'Age?'

'Hard to say. He looked about mid-forties but something about the way he walked made him seem older. He sort of stooped a bit.'

'Interesting,' Highwater said pensively.

'Would you recognise him if you saw him again?' Gemma asked, folding her arms and cocking her head to one side.

'In a moment, Agent X-ray,' Barney nodded, tapping his temple. 'Every detail of that dude is filed away in my photographic memory. With my perfect recall I'd remember him even if I saw him in ten years' time. And I'm talking tiny details – not just his blue cagoule . . .'

'Green,' whispered Archie.

'Sorry?'

'His cagoule was green, not blue.'

'Really?' Barney frowned. 'I could have sworn it was blue. Maybe it was a sort of bluey-green?'

Archie shook his head almost imperceptibly.

26

'Anyway,' Highwater said, bringing the dispute to an end. 'It's good to know you would recognise this man if you ever met him again. Forewarned is forearmed. If you provide Intel Branch with a full description they can run a search on the database.'

'Do any suspects spring to mind?' Archie asked.

Highwater nodded grimly. 'One in particular. Sounds like you followed protocol to the letter though. Any time you're pursued by a potential hostile it is imperative that you evade and shelter.'

A series of high-pitched beeps from the other side of the door signalled someone typing the entry code into the hidden keypad.

Six bleeps, a pause then a clunk and the door opened outward. In walked an elderly man in a tweed jacket with the sleeves pushed up to his bony elbows. He had a thin white moustache and his fine silvery hair was gelled up into a quiff at the front.

Holden Grey was STINKBOMB's experienced Tech Branch Specialist. Having retired from MI6 twenty-odd years ago his technological knowledge was hardly up to date but he had returned to active duty to kit out Agents X-ray, Yankee and Zulu for their mission to track down Dr Doom. Keen for the young agents to like him, he was desperate to show them he wasn't too old to be cool.

'Hey, posse,' he said brightly, his eager blue eyes pausing on each of the kids in turn. 'What's going downwards?'

'Hello, Mr Grey,' the three children replied together, a note of amused affection in their voices. The old man high-fived each of them in turn.

'Where have you been?' Highwater asked in her customary curt manner.

'Upstairs, in the kitchen,' Grey replied. 'Just making a snack. I've been so busy in the workshop since nine a.m. I forgot all about lunch. A chap, I mean a dog, can't think straight on an empty stomach, you feel me?'

'Quite right, Mr Grey,' said Highwater. 'Anyway, you're just in time – I was about to brief the team on Operation Gumshield.'

Archie felt his spine tingle at the mention of a new mission. Over the last six months he'd spent most of his spare time secretly learning spy tradecraft and he was excited about putting his training into action.

Helen Highwater waited while Holden Grey took up his usual position, standing at her shoulder, then she began. 'As you may already know, next weekend the

28

British Student Games are being held in London. The athletics will take place in Crystal Palace and there'll be a swimming gala at the K2 in Crawley as well as rowing at Dorney Lake. But your only concern is that on Saturday this young man will be competing in the boxing at the O2 Arena.'

Holden Grey unfolded his spindly arms and pointed a remote control at one of the wall-mounted monitors. A picture of a boy filled the screen. He looked about fifteen years old, with cropped blond hair and a strong jaw line.

'Who is he?' asked Barney.

'He's *fine*,' enthused Gemma.

'I don't know,' Archie mumbled casually. 'He looks like a meathead to me.'

'He is Toby Winchester,' announced Highwater. 'Son of Adam Winchester – our very own Prime Minister.'

'Ordinarily these games wouldn't make the headlines,' Grey added. 'But Toby Winchester's involvement ensures the ears of the world will be watching very closely indeed.'

'MI5 and MI6 will be running a joint operation at the event,' Highwater explained. 'There will be a huge uniformed presence, as well as scores of undercover

29

agents covering every conceivable angle, be it terrorist attack, kidnap attempt or even just some wacko looking for attention.'

'So what do you need us for?' asked Archie.

'We need you three to be on the inside, mixing with the athletes,' said Highwater. 'As kids you can get closer to Toby Winchester than any adult MI6 agents. We want you to watch him closely – twenty-four-seven.'

'You got it,' said Gemma. 'I won't take my eyes off him. That's a promise.'

As Holden Grey strode across to one of the laptops, his shoes squeaked on the marble floor. Archie looked down instinctively and saw the old man was wearing a spotless pair of bright white Nike basketball boots with the thick orange laces left untied. The old man tapped a couple of keys and an inkjet printer whirred into life at the end of the counter. Retrieving three sheets of paper from the printer he handed one to each of the agents.

'These are your undercover identities,' Highwater informed them. 'You are to memorise the profiles until the information is second nature. Mistakes can cost lives.'

'Wicked,' cooed Barney, his hand trembling as he studied his sheet.

30

Grey stroked his moustache pensively and said, 'BWT, guys, these profiles are FYOE, aka for your eyes only.'

'We'll rendezvous here next Friday after school,' Highwater announced. 'Your cover stories will be tested so make sure you're up to speed. The boxing competition is scheduled to take place over the weekend. On Saturday we'll travel to London early – get you all embedded in your roles before the games begin.'

'So I have to come all the way down here again next Friday?' Gemma groaned, folding her arms. 'Why can't Yankee and Zulu come up to London instead?'

Helen Highwater removed her glasses and studied the young girl for a moment. 'Agent X-ray,' she said coldly. 'The locations of our meetings are decided by me, and me alone. I'm sorry that you consider travelling to this safe house to be so inconvenient but its location on the south coast makes it ideal for our covert operations. Apart from not attracting the attention of hostile organisations – and I include the national press in that category – STINKBOMB can operate from this base without the continuous scrutiny of MI6 central command. Essentially it gives us almost total autonomy as an agency and for that alone I'd have thought the hassle of your train journey was a small price to pay. Do I make myself clear?'

Gemma's jaw jutted forward slightly but she said nothing, nodding once, slowly.

'Besides, all my gear is here,' added Grey jovially. 'And I've got a couple of fierce gadgets that should be ready in time for your assignment.'

Barney barely suppressed a yelp of delight but Archie's mind was elsewhere. Something had been niggling him for the last few minutes and he'd suddenly realised what it was. His heart was pounding as adrenalin coursed through his body.

'Agent Yankee,' said Highwater. 'Do you have anything you wish to add?'

He was sure he was right, yet the prospect of making a fool of himself had kept his mouth shut.

'Agent Yankee!' Highwater repeated irately.

Archie felt his conviction swelling like a balloon inside him. If he was wrong he would look stupid for a while, but if he was right and said nothing he would never forgive himself.

'It was you.' His nervousness pushed the words out more forcefully than he'd intended. Pointing at Holden Grey, he took a calming breath and said, 'You were the man in the green cagoule. You were following us in the shops.'

A chilled silence filled the room.

All eyes were on Archie.

'Agent Yankee, that is an extraordinary accusation,' said Highwater. 'I think you'd better explain yourself. And it had better be good.'

Chapter 5

Archie immediately regretted airing his suspicions in front of everyone. Perhaps a quiet word with Helen Highwater would have been a more tactful way of expressing his concerns but it was too late for that.

Eight eyes scrutinised him as he took a moment to mentally organise his evidence.

'OK,' he said, his voice barely a croak. After clearing his throat he started again. 'OK. The man following us was about six feet tall and weighed about a hundred and forty pounds. I estimate Mr Grey fits that description pretty closely.'

'Mr Grey?' Highwater enquired.

'I must say I find Agent Yankee's insinuation most outrageous. It's totally whacked.' Holden Grey's eyes narrowed. 'It just so happens I'm six feet exactly in my socks and a hundred and forty three pounds.'

'This proves only that you can evaluate physiques with reasonable accuracy.' Highwater sat back in her chair. 'I'm sure many thousands of men in this country fit that profile.'

'Mr Grey's posture matches the man who followed us too.'

'Lots of people of Mr Grey's age experience slight curvature of the spine,' Highwater stated.

Archie conceded the point with a nod, then countered, 'But how many of those men wear brown corduroy trousers?'

Helen Highwater remained unimpressed. 'I hardly think his possession of a pair of brown cords is conclusive evidence that Mr Grey followed you this morning.' Sitting forward, she leaned her elbows on her desk and rested her fingertips together. 'I do hope you've got something more substantial to back up your theory, Agent Yankee.'

Archie felt his confidence wobble. He'd expected Highwater to find his evidence so far much more convincing. He took a moment to gather his thoughts.

'Agent Yankee,' Highwater barked. 'We're all waiting.'

'I suppose you're right,' Archie said with a shrug. 'Lots of men share Mr Grey's build and posture as well as his taste in trousers. And the man who followed us was obviously wearing a false moustache and probably a wig so it's almost impossible to identify the culprit facially.'

'Are you now saying you're *not* sure it was me following you?' asked Grey, a hint of pleasure in his voice.

'No.' Archie shook his head slowly. 'I'm saying that my reasons for suspecting you are nothing to do with your choice of trousers but everything to do with the state your trousers are in.'

'Man, you'd better be sure of your stuff,' chuckled Gemma.

Archie took a deep breath. 'I couldn't help noticing that the hems of Mr Grey's trousers are spattered with muddy water. I know that, as a man with exceptional personal standards, you would never put on muddy trousers in the morning. Which means you must have splashed them some time today.'

Grey smiled easily. 'I must have stepped in a puddle on my way here this morning.'

'But it didn't start raining today until eleven a.m. and

we haven't had any rain before that for a week.'

'So I must have come into work a little later than usual? My badly.'

'But a few moments ago you said that you'd been in the workshop since nine a.m.' It was Archie's turn to enjoy an easy smile. 'If you'd been here since then, your trousers would be bone dry.'

Barney gasped.

Highwater sat back and folded her arms. 'Agent Yankee,' she said, giving Archie a saccharine smile. 'If what you are saying is true, then surely I would be aware of Mr Grey's movements. I have been here all day, as has Agent X-ray.'

'Exactly,' Archie grinned. 'You weren't surprised to see us in the least. In fact you seemed to be expecting us because you were already prepared to brief us on Operation Gumshield. We weren't scheduled to come here today but you knew that when we realised we were being followed we would evade and shelter, which means we'd come scurrying to this safe house.'

'Agent Zulu?' Highwater enquired, removing her glasses to hold Barney's gaze. 'Do you share Agent Yankee's conspiracy theory – remembering of course that any false accusation made against a member of

37

Her Majesty's Secret Service could be construed as treasonous?'

Barney looked bewildered, like someone trying to work out a brilliant magician's card trick. Leaning towards Archie he murmured through the corner of his mouth, 'Just run that bit about the muddy trousers past me again.'

Cupping his hand around his friend's ear, Archie whispered an explanation during which Barney's eyes grew steadily wider like a pair of balloons inflating. When Archie had finished his recap, Barney stared at Holden Grey, then Helen Highwater, his mouth an open circle of disbelief. 'I don't believe it!' he gasped, quickly adding, 'I mean, er, I concur with Agent Yankee's assessment, having noticed many of the same inconsistencies myself and reached the same conclusion.'

'I see.' Helen Highwater sat back in her leather chair and sighed gravely. Pressing her palms together she considered both boys carefully.

Archie's legs felt like jelly as he waited for her reaction.

After a moment Highwater began to applaud. 'Congratulations,' she said sternly. 'You effectively evaded Mr Grey in the field and you identified the suspect using a combination of recollection and lateral thinking.'

'So this was all just a test?' asked Archie, a feeling of relief flushing through his limbs.

'Yeah.' Agent X-ray smiled. 'You were more like lab rats than blind mice.'

'Operation Gumshield is a high profile mission,' Highwater stated. 'We can't afford any slip-ups when the PM's son is involved. I knew you were ready for field ops but my boss, Huge Ego – I mean Hugh Figo – wanted proof that your surveillance and counter-surveillance skills are up to scratch.'

'Well done, your bad selves,' added Holden Grey.

'Would we really have been charged with treason if we'd been wrong?' Archie asked, pushing his glasses up his nose.

'Goodness me, no!' Grey chuckled. 'We just wanted to see if you would have the courage of your guns and stick to your convictions.'

'I expect my STINKBOMB agents to trust their instincts,' Highwater added. 'Regardless of the consequences.'

Archie and Barney nodded.

'OK, before we run through some of the plans for Operation Gumshield, does anyone have any questions?'

'Er, yes,' Barney mumbled. 'I was wondering if Mr Grey retrieved our decoy garments from the field and if so could we have them back?'

'If you're referring to your hoodies, then yes I did,' said Holden Grey. 'They're upstairs – I'll go and get them now. Be back in a mojo.'

'You're not cold, are you?' Archie enquired.

Barney shook his head. 'Not cold – hungry. I left my Picnic in my pocket.'

'Can't believe a pair of dummies gave Mr Grey the slip.' Gemma said with a smirk. 'And I don't mean the ones in the shop.'

Chapter 6

Archie was sitting at the vast table in the vast kitchen of the vast house he lived in with his father, millionaire aviator Richard Hunt. He liked their home – it was pretty cool, with loads of gadgets and close to the coast – but sometimes it felt too big. When his mother was alive the house had always seemed cosier somehow. Without her there was just a bit too much space.

Archie's mother had died nearly four years ago, but he still thought about her every day. Often something would trigger a specific memory and, for a heartbeat, it would feel like she was still alive, before the memory disappeared like smoke.

Archie's mind drifted, settling on Yuri Villenemi, the evil mastermind responsible for his mother's death, whom STINKBOMB had been tasked with finding on their maiden mission. Until he had come face to face with Villenemi, Archie had believed his mother was a regular mum, but the arch villain had taken great pleasure in revealing the truth. Lara Hunt had been an undercover MI6 agent. When she'd attempted to track Villenemi down, he had killed her in cold blood before faking his own death.

Six months ago Villenemi had resurfaced, calling himself Dr Doom, and kidnapped Archie's father as part of his plot to take over the world. It had been down to Archie, Barney and Gemma to rescue Richard Hunt and thwart Doom's evil plan, and Archie was incredibly proud that they had succeeded in their first assignment.

It meant the world to him to be part of STINKBOMB – not just because they were protecting national security but also because he was following in his mother's footsteps. He was carrying on the work that she had sacrificed her life for. With a twinge of sadness he wondered how she would have felt about his role in STINKBOMB.

Archie knew he had inherited his mother's natural flair for languages and her aptitude for martial arts, but he often speculated whether he shared any other characteristics with her. And would she have ever revealed the truth about her job? Archie sighed. The fact that he would never know the answers, and that he would always miss her, was the hardest thing of all.

'Hey, kiddo.'

Archie's father ruffled his hair.

'Morning, Dad.'

Richard Hunt marched briskly into the room and turned the radio down. 'I don't know how you can hear yourself think with that racket going on,' he said, draining his coffee mug and placing it on the table. Dressed in jeans and a light blue sweater he looked strong and lean, the grey flecks at the sides of his thick dark hair the only evidence that he was heading for his fifties.

'What's happening today?' he asked, scanning the kitchen.

Archie looked at his father for a moment, then said, 'In an exciting change to my usual schedule, today I'm going to *school*.'

Spotting what he was after, Richard Hunt grabbed a leather documents folder. 'I meant what lessons have you got?'

'Well, after lunch I expect Mr Jackson will send us

all to sleep with some algebra. But this morning I think Moore the Bore's going to suck all the life out of us during double history.'

'I thought she taught biology?'

'Oh, she's multi-talented,' Archie enthused. 'She can make either subject as much fun as having a filling.'

'No wonder they say these are the best days of your life.' Archie's dad winked.

'Dad,' Archie groaned. 'Please don't say that, it's so depressing.'

'Nothing exciting happening outside of school?' Richard Hunt asked. 'No new EMUs on STINKBOMB's radar?'

Archie shrugged. 'Actually we've got an assignment at the weekend.'

Richard Hunt studied his son, a hint of concern creasing his forehead. 'What's the mission?'

'It's nothing very exciting. We're going undercover at the British Student Games in London. It's just a routine surveillance op.'

Richard Hunt's eyes narrowed. 'There's no such thing as a *routine* surveillance op,' he said sternly. 'You never know when things are going to get dicey. You have to keep your wits about you at all times. Just because you beat the bad guys in your first assignment doesn't mean you can afford to get cocky on this one.'

'Dad, relax.' Archie smiled reassuringly. 'I'm not getting cocky, honestly. I'll be careful – I promise.'

Archie's father pursed his lips. 'Sorry, kiddo. I know you will, I just can't help worrying about you.'

'I know, Dad.' Archie nodded. 'But this won't be as dangerous as the first mission. I mean, for starters, you haven't got yourself kidnapped this time so I won't have to risk my life saving your skin.'

'Touché!' Richard Hunt laughed. 'Are you ever going to stop reminding me that you saved my life?'

Archie considered his response for a moment. 'Not in a million years.'

'Thought not,' Richard replied. 'Listen, I've got to go – we're donating two Dragonflies to the Global Disaster Relief Organisation and I'm making the presentation today.'

Since leaving the Air Force Archie's father had designed and produced a four-seater jet aircraft that was capable of hovering, as well as performing a vertical take-off and landing. The Dragonfly had proved popular with wealthy businessmen and aid agencies alike.

Shortly after Archie's tenth birthday, Richard had

begun to let him take the controls of the Dragonfly. Archie had inherited his father's passion and talent for flying and he had quickly become an accomplished aviator.

Richard Hunt kissed the top of his son's forehead and headed for the door. 'See you later. And don't have too much fun at school.'

'As if,' Archie grumbled. As his father opened the door to leave Archie piped up. 'Dad, do you ever feel like this house is too big?'

Richard Hunt stopped and turned, observing his son for a moment before smiling kindly. 'Every day, kiddo,' he said. 'Every day.'

Archie nodded and managed a smile. 'See you later, Dad.'

When the door closed Archie stared out of the window at the sea beyond. 'White male, mid-forties,' he said aloud, practising his observational recollection. 'Dark hair, grey at the temples, parted on the left. Pale blue jumper, Paul Smith jeans and Oxford brogues – reddish brown.' He closed his eyes, trying to recall any other details. 'Breitling watch on his left wrist, bright red socks and he's wearing that fancy aftershave he likes.'

Archie inhaled the familiar scent deeply through his nose and smiled. Then, with a small sigh, he pushed his chair back, grabbed his parka and his rucksack and headed for the door.

Archie scuffed his shoes along the damp pavement as he made his way to school from the bus stop. The dreary sky matched his mood. He didn't normally mind school – even quite enjoyed it sometimes – and he couldn't quite work out why he felt so negative about everything this morning. Things weren't so bad, he thought, trying to lift his own spirits. There'd be time to chat to Barney at lunch break and he had swimming after school. And there were only five days before the weekend – when STINKBOMB's second assignment would begin. Archie couldn't wait!

Suddenly someone shoved him hard in the back. As Archie stumbled forward he felt his rucksack being yanked off his shoulder and his glasses fell on to the ground. As he crouched to retrieve them a hefty school shoe pressed against his ribs and pushed him backwards. Losing his balance, Archie toppled on to his bottom and sat in a cold puddle, which quickly seeped through his trousers to his underpants.

47

'Hardly Human, what a surprise,' Archie said flatly. 'I would never have thought it was you.'

'What's my name?' demanded the sturdy kid standing over Archie.

'You haven't forgotten again, have you?' Archie asked innocently, wiping the mud off his spectacles and sliding them on. 'Check your clothes – I expect your mummy labelled them for you.'

'It's Harvey Newman,' the boy snarled.

'Well why were you asking me if you knew all along?' Archie clambered to his feet.

Newman shoved Archie in the chest. 'You called me Hardly Human. I don't like being called that.'

'Whereas I love being shoved over for no reason,' Archie mumbled.

Wearing just his shirt, sleeves rolled up and his tie pulled loose, Newman's arms were pink and ripe, like shoulders of pork. He snorted like a pig. 'That was pretty funny,' he said, looking to his three gormless sidekicks who all grinned and nodded. 'We just thought we'd surprise you before school.'

'Brilliant.' Archie smiled sarcastically. 'Can I have my rucksack back now? Please.'

'Of course you can.' Newman grinned, unzipping

the bag. 'I just want to show you that it's all here – just in case you were worrying that we might have nicked something.'

Archie could sense what Newman was about to do and thought about reminding him what he was capable of. Newman's stance was pretty narrow, leaving him susceptible to having his feet swept from under him. Archie would follow up the sweep with a jab to the solar plexus, which would wind Newman just enough to deter him from retaliation.

But Archie remained motionless. His personal code prevented him from using his martial arts skills unless he was in grave personal danger and, although frustrating, having his school books tipped on to the ground was not about to kill him. Besides, his cover as a STINKBOMB agent was strengthened by the fact that everyone at school thought he was a total wimp.

'Please don't tip my stuff out,' Archie said plaintively.

Newman chuckled but, just as he was about to upend the rucksack, he was interrupted by a voice from his right.

'Put the bag down, Newman!' commanded Barney, approaching slowly with his palms up. 'Place the bag on the floor and step away.'

Newman stopped and stared at Barney, narrowing his eyes and smirking nastily.

'This is none of your business, Chubs,' Newman sneered. 'Why don't you waddle off and get yourself a cake or something?'

'It's OK, Barney,' Archie whispered. 'I'll be fine.'

'I'm making it my business,' Barney retorted, ignoring Archie's protests. 'If you bully him, you bully me.'

Newman screwed his face up. 'What does that mean?' he sniffed.

Calmly Barney said, 'If you tip Archie's rucksack out, then you'd better be ready to tip mine out too.'

'Oh, right,' Newman replied. 'Well why didn't you say so?'

'Is this your rubber or mine?' Archie asked.

'Let's have a look,' said Barney. 'Must be yours. Mine had James Bond on it.'

'Cool.' Archie dropped the rubber into his pencil case, zipped it up and tossed it into his rucksack.

The two boys were sitting on their heels scrabbling at the contents of both their bags, which Harvey Newman had gleefully emptied on to the wet ground.

'I did suggest you shouldn't get involved,' Archie muttered.

'I saw an agent in a tight spot,' Barney explained. 'I was just providing back-up.'

'Well you certainly got Newman's back up,' Archie giggled. As he reached for his sodden maths textbook he noticed a pair of black suede women's boots in front of him. When his eyes trailed upward he saw the person in the boots was wearing a black skirt and a cream woollen coat. Her shoulder-length hair was parted in the middle and curled slightly at the ends, softening the frame of her pointed face.

'Are you OK, boys?' she asked kindly. 'I think the bell's about to go.'

Archie swiftly stood up, smiling. 'Everything's fine, thank you,' he said. He assumed the lady was a teacher, although he didn't recognise her.

'What class have you got this morning?' she asked.

'History with Moore the B— I mean Miss Moore,' Archie replied, his last word accompanied by the drill of the school bell.

'Oh man, we're late,' Barney sighed, standing up. 'We're going to get detention for sure.'

'Oh I don't know about that,' the woman replied

with a faint smile. 'If you hurry I reckon you'll be behind your desks before your teacher even gets to the classroom.'

'No chance,' Archie muttered, slinging his rucksack over his shoulder. 'Moore is *never* late.'

Archie and Barney sprinted through the school gates, pushed open the double entrance doors and jogged the length of B-Block corridor. They paused outside their classroom to hang up their coats and catch their breath before the verbal tirade that was coming their way.

'We are so dead,' Barney whispered.

'I know,' Archie replied. 'It was nice knowing you.'

Then he pushed open the door to the classroom.

Chapter 7

Everyone in the class stared in silence as Archie and Barney entered. Archie looked instinctively to the seat behind the desk at the front of the class, normally occupied by his teacher. But it was empty. Then he scanned the perimeter of the room before checking the identity of each and every person who sat facing him.

'Where's Moore?' Barney asked the class.

One voice rose above the hubbub of muttered 'dunnos'.

'You two are so jammy,' Harvey Newman groaned. 'I can't believe Moore the Bore's not here to see you coming in late.'

Archie and Barney quickly took their seats, just as the classroom door opened and a woman in her late thirties walked in. She smiled brightly as she draped her cream coat over her chair and placed her grey crocodile skin handbag on the desk.

'Good morning, everyone,' she announced, hooking her hair behind her ears. 'My name is Miss Toogood. Unfortunately Miss Moore broke her arm at the weekend and will be off work for a few months. I will be covering her classes and I'm really looking forward to meeting all of you. It's so nice to see you all sitting down so promptly, ready to learn.'

An awed silence descended over the classroom. The arrival of a supply teacher was usually an invitation for the class to mess around without fear of reprisal – but something about Miss Toogood's controlled manner commanded respect.

'Actually, Archie Hunt and Barney Jones were late today, miss,' Harvey Newman whined.

'Thank you, Mr . . . ?'

'Newman, miss. Harvey Newman.'

'Where are Messrs Hunt and Jones?' the teacher demanded.

Archie and Barney sheepishly raised their hands. Miss Toogood surveyed the boys briefly before addressing Newman. 'Well, Harvey, I can see you are someone I

54

can rely on to follow the rules to the letter,' she said warmly. 'But as far as I can tell, Archie and Barney are here in plenty of time for the class.'

Archie half turned and grinned over his shoulder. Harvey Newman snarled.

'So this morning we'll be learning about history,' Miss Toogood announced.

The class responded with a weary groan.

'I love the enthusiasm!' the teacher joked. 'Why is everyone so down on history lessons?'

The class fell silent, no one wanting to be the first to answer, and then Harvey Newman shouted out, 'Cos it's boring, isn't it?'

The response to Newman's comment was mixed. Some kids gasped while others tittered nervously as they awaited the teacher's reaction. Miss Toogood milked the tension for a moment, then she smiled. 'OK, Harvey. Can you explain why it's so boring?'

Newman shrugged. His cheeks coloured, then he said, 'It's all just old news, isn't it?'

'I see. Does anybody else have an idea as to why we might find history lessons a little bit dull?'

Holly Jenkins, a slender girl with braces and pigtails, put her hand up. 'It's just really hard for us to, like, get our heads round, like, all those big political meetings and, you know, conferences and stuff?'

'OK.' Miss Toogood clicked her fingers, her eyes twinkling. 'I agree it can be hard to see the relevance of events that happened years ago. And I understand that learning about complicated political decision-making processes can seem very confusing. But what I want to demonstrate is that there is no difference between diplomacy at the highest level and what goes on in the classrooms today.'

'Are you saying all the Prime Ministers have to sit through double maths?' laughed Newman.

Miss Toogood smiled. 'Not exactly, Harvey. I suppose the best way of explaining what I mean is by way of analogy. Let's assume—'

'Sorry?' Newman exclaimed, an exaggerated expression of surprise on his face. 'Did you say *an allergy*? I think I might have an allergy to history if that's what you mean!'

Newman cast his eyes around the room. One or two classmates giggled.

'I can see you're quite the comedian, Harvey.' Miss Toogood smiled sweetly – then her tone hardened. 'But if you ever interrupt me or any of your classmates again I will have you cleaning out the toilet block every lunch hour for a month. Is that clear?'

Newman hung his head and nodded.

'As I was saying,' Miss Toogood continued, 'for our analogy let's assume I am like the United Nations Security Council and you are all individual countries. Now what if I saw the country of, say, Newmania bullying the smaller state of Huntingdon? What options would I have open to me?'

Archie raised his hand. 'You might give Newmania a warning.'

'Exactly. Like a teacher telling off a child I would let Newmania know that if it didn't stop bullying its neighbouring state, then further action would be taken. Can anyone tell me what that action might be?'

'You could stop Newmania trading with other states?' suggested Brandon Hutt.

'Precisely. In the political world the withdrawal of certain privileges is known as imposing sanctions,' Miss Toogood replied. 'It's the classroom equivalent of handing out detention or litter duty. And if Newmania persisted in misbehaving?'

'As a last resort you'd have the military option,' suggested Barney.

57

'Exactly,' Miss Toogood said with relish, a gleeful glint in her eye. 'If the sanctions failed to have any impact I'd immediately respond with immense power and ferocity. When my destructive rampage was over, Mr Newman would be physically and mentally crushed and regret the day he ever dreamed of crossing me.'

Silence engulfed the room for a few seconds, then Archie cleared his throat. 'I think you mean Newmania, miss,' he said quietly.

Unclenching her fists, Miss Toogood turned to Archie and smiled. 'I'm sorry?'

'You said you'd crush Mr Newman,' Archie said tentatively. 'But I think you meant to say, hypothetically, you'd crush the state of Newmania.'

'Oh yes, of course,' Miss Toogood said softly, hooking her hair behind her ear. 'Silly me.'

58

Chapter 8

It had been a long slow week but at four thirty on Friday afternoon Archie and Barney stood outside the front door of 16 Stour Gardens. Archie was wearing jeans and trainers, a red Hollister hoody and a sleeveless blue puffer. Barney was dressed in combats, polo neck, nylon bomber jacket, gloves and beanie hat – all in black.

Archie paused as he reached for the doorbell and regarded his friend. 'You do know we're here just to brief a mission, right?'

Barney nodded, all business.

'An *undercover surveillance* operation.' The corners of Archie's mouth twitched as he continued. 'And as far as I know we're pretty unlikely to end up storming an embassy or anything.'

Barney's head turned to Archie like an automaton. 'Copy that,' he replied.

Archie frowned slightly and pressed the doorbell.

Numerous clunks sounded as the internal bolts on the door were released, then it opened six inches, until the security chain was yanked taut. Gemma peered through the narrow opening, one eyebrow raised, and said, 'Girls go to college to get more knowledge.'

'Come on, Gem,' Archie complained, his inadvertent shortening of her name making him blush.

Gemma sternly repeated her part of the passcode sequence.

'OK, have it your way,' Archie sighed. 'Boys go to Jupiter to get more stupider.'

The door closed momentarily, then opened wide. Gemma grinned at Archie and Barney as she gestured them into the house. She looked Barney up and down. 'I'm loving the outfit, Zulu,' she enthused. 'As usual you're blending right in. What's in the bag?'

'Operationally essential items.' Barney patted his rucksack. 'Notepad, camera, Monster Munch, mobile phone, family pack of Kit Kats.'

'Well at least you won't starve,' said Gemma. 'Are you ready for the brief?'

Barney smirked. 'Do mongooses fly south for the winter?'

Gemma pulled a face. 'O-K. I'll take that as a yes.'

Archie leaned towards Barney and cupped a hand to his mouth. 'You do know that a mongoose isn't a bird, don't you?'

Barney's eyes narrowed slightly. 'Really? I mean, sure,' he babbled. 'It's a kind of small fox, right? Or a cat?'

'It's a rodent.'

'Exactly,' Barney nodded vigorously. 'A sort of foxy cat-type rodent.'

Archie smiled and turned to Gemma, 'You got here early. How was the journey?'

'All right, considering,' she shrugged. 'I had to skip double physics, so sitting on the train was actually a bonus. My mum told the school I had a dental appointment.'

'Your parents know you're an agent?' Barney asked.

'Er . . . obviously.' Gemma pulled a face. 'They had to sign all the papers to say I could do the training and go on missions. Yours must have signed them too, right?'

'Of course.' Barney frowned seriously, then pursed his lips uncertainly. 'I'm just not sure they took them that seriously. I've got a feeling they thought I'd printed all the forms off the Internet and they signed them just to humour me.'

'That's so weird,' Archie commented. 'Why would they imagine you're the sort of person who'd fantasise about working for MI6? I mean it's not like you're a total James Bond fanatic who's been obsessed with spy fiction since before he could talk. Oh, wait a minute . . .' He clicked his fingers. 'That's exactly the sort of person you are.'

'So, geekily having played secret agents your whole life is the perfect cover story for being a real agent.' Gemma smiled. 'It's actually brilliant. I'd be impressed if I didn't know you.'

Barney shrugged modestly. 'Understood.'

'OK, let's go to the Ops Room,' Gemma suggested. 'It's best not to keep IC waiting.'

The boys followed Gemma down to the fortified basement. Helen Highwater was sitting behind her desk and at her shoulder stood Holden Grey, who was wearing a thick burgundy hoody.

'Good afternoon, Yankee . . . and Zulu.' Highwater curtly nodded in turn at Archie and Barney, who each nodded back.

'Wassup!' Holden Grey double-tapped his own chest with his fist, immediately letting out a wheezy cough. 'It's the STINKBOMB posse in the home.'

The three children smiled. 'I think you mean "in the house", Mr Grey,' Archie suggested.

Helen Highwater cleared her throat. 'Shall we get down to business then?'

'OK, guys,' said Grey. 'Just to reiterate once more – from the moment you go undercover you must stay in character. You will maintain your persona non grata at all times and by that I mean . . . er . . . at all times. Capiche?'

'Capiche,' Archie replied while his co-agents nodded.

'Your stories have to be absolutely watertight,' Grey continued. 'Otherwise they won't hold water and you'll be sunk. Not that something that's full of water would float anyway – unless the volume of the vessel's walls was greater than the volume of water it contained and it was constructed of a material that was less dense than water. Like polystyrene or indeed any number of poly—'

'I think that's quite enough of the Archimedes principle for now, thank you, Mr Grey,' said Highwater sternly. Addressing the agents, she continued, 'OK, team. As discussed last weekend, tomorrow you will all be running undercover ops at the British Student Games. The purpose of Operation Gumshield is to protect Toby Winchester, the PM's son, who is competing in the boxing tournament. Firstly, you will achieve this by watching Toby closely. Secondly, and possibly more importantly, you will blend in with the competitors and officials at the event and report any suspicious activity among them. I trust you've all studied your undercover identities? I'm going to test you by asking a few simple questions that I want you to answer as your alter ego. I want you all to remain in character until I tell you otherwise.' Highwater pointed at Gemma.

'Hi, what's your name?' she asked pleasantly.

'Vanessa Wallis.'

'Where are you from?'

'Just up the road. Stratford.'

'When's your birthday?'

'Twenty-ninth of January.'

'That must make you a Pisces?'

'Nah – Aquarius.'

'What are you doing here?'

Gemma shrugged uninterestedly. 'I'm with St John's.'

'The ambulance service?'

'No, the world famous St John's Acrobatic Troupe.' Gemma snorted sardonically.

'I'll have less of your sarcasm if you don't mind, Agent X-ray,' Highwater snapped.

Gemma narrowed her eyes and held her boss's stare. 'Who's Agent X-ray?' she asked innocently.

Archie was transfixed by Highwater's expression. He felt slightly sick with nerves as he waited for her to explode. The muscles in her jaw flexed as she ground her teeth together and then took a long deep breath. 'It's very nice to meet you, Vanessa,' she said coolly. Turning to Barney, Highwater beamed. 'Hello, Agent Zulu.'

Barney grinned and said, 'Hello, IC.'

'You're supposed to be in character,' Highwater sighed. 'Let's start again. What's your name?'

'My name is Luke Sharpe,' Barney recited. 'I live in Windsor with my parents, a cat, and two fish. I am a journalist on the kids' magazine *Newshound* and I am here to cover the British Student Games in an informative and accessible style. My favourite film is *Anchorman* although I don't feel it's an accurate reflection on the world of journalism and when I grow up I'd like to write for the *Daily Mail*. I'm into music, sci-fi and gaming.'

Highwater rolled her eyes. 'Just remember you're having a conversation, not speed dating. Less is more.'

'Copy that.'

'What's your cat called?'

'Er . . .' A look of panic swelled in Barney's eyes. 'Mr – um – ginger – tabby – puss?'

'Mr Gingertabbypuss?' Highwater repeated incredulously.

'Yeah.' Barney swallowed hard. 'He's a cross.'

'Well I think I'd be cross if I was called Mr Gingertabbypuss,' Highwater drawled. Her mouth curved downward as she considered her next remark. After a few moments she spoke in a whisper. 'If you are going to be a member of my team it is imperative that you do your homework – do I make myself clear?'

Barney nodded eagerly.

'It clearly states in your brief that your cat's name, ironically, is Einstein.'

'Copy that.'

'And stop saying "copy that" – you sound like someone on a SWAT team! You're supposed to be a journalist.'

'OK,' Barney agreed uncertainly. 'Then . . . hold the front page.'

Highwater folded her arms on her desk and allowed her forehead to drop on to her wrists.

'All you need to remember,' suggested Holden Grey gently, 'is to keep everything simple. Don't volunteer information and don't say anything contradictory.'

'Better still,' said Highwater, lifting her head wearily, 'don't say anything at all.' She flicked through some pages on her desk. 'OK, Yankee,' she announced. 'Let's see how much of your cover you've memorised.'

Suddenly nervous, Archie rubbed his clammy palms on his jeans as he waited for his interrogation to begin.

'Actually, Mr Grey, could you interrogate Yankee for me?' Highwater sighed, sitting upright and pinching the top of her nose. 'I can feel a headache coming on.'

'No problematico,' replied Grey enthusiastically, tugging back the sleeves of his hooded top. Holding a fist out to Archie he said, 'Hey, dude! What's your name, my man?'

'Hook,' said Archie, bumping his fist against Grey's. 'Daniel Hook.'

'Where's your hood?'

'I'm from Upminster – Essex.'

'What do you think of the new Black Eyed Peas record? It's enormously wicked, do you hear me?'

'I'm all over it, man,' said Archie.

'I can hear you. So is you spectatoring today?'

Archie shook his head. 'I'm boxing for the South of England.'

'That's well cold isn't it? Which category are you fighting in?'

'Junior light-middle.'

'Me too! I'm on the North of England team.' Grey held out his fist again and Archie bumped it.

'When's your birthday, dude?' Grey continued his questioning.

'April thirtieth.'

'You into the football?'

'I can take it or leave it.'

'What school did you say you go to?'

'I didn't.'

'I hear Toby Winchester is competing today.'

'Never heard of him.'

After the quick-fire exchange the room almost hummed with silence. Archie waited for Grey's next advance, like a fencer waiting for his opponent to attack. But Grey just smiled. 'Good work, Archie.'

'Thank you, Mr Grey.' Archie grinned but immediately saw the expression of disappointment in the old man's eyes and knew he had blown his cover.

'Nice try, Yankee.' said Highwater. 'But you must, must, *must* maintain your cover story at all times. Even if you think it's safe to drop it. Always assume someone can hear you or see you. Is that clear?'

Archie nodded glumly, feeling frustrated with himself. He knew better than to fall for such a simple trick and he would have to raise his game during Operation Gumshield. Out in the field such a careless mistake could put the lives of his fellow agents, and Toby Winchester, in grave danger.

Chapter 9

'Well done, X-ray,' congratulated Highwater.

Gemma smiled proudly.

'And Zulu . . . ' Highwater continued, 'I suggest you consider making Luke Sharpe a mute. Then at least you can't say anything to incriminate yourself.'

'But then I couldn't ask any journalistic questions,' Barney observed, taking his boss seriously.

'Precisely,' Highwater said, pursing her lips and puffing out her cheeks. 'Maybe we'll make you a photo journalist instead. Your brief is to say nothing – photograph everything.'

'I can definitely do that.' Barney beamed.

'Good, let's leave it at that.' Highwater placed her palms on her desk, pushed her chair back and stood up. 'Now there's one more thing I want to show you before Mr Grey talks you through your specialist equipment.'

'I think being a photographer is a cool cover,' Archie whispered to his friend. 'It *lens* itself really well to covert surveillance.'

'I'll shoot on sight,' Barney nodded. 'And if I see something unusual I'll put IC in the picture.'

Archie smiled. 'It'll be interesting to see what develops.'

'It's a lot of pressure though. I hope I don't snap.'

'Er – I don't think this is the time for camera jokes,' Gemma hissed, rolling her eyes. 'For heaven's sake just try and *focus*.'

Highwater picked up a remote control and one of the many flat-screen monitors lining the walls flickered into life, showing an image of a pretty young woman. She had long flame-coloured hair and milky white skin. Her features were small and her jawline slender. Highwater cleared her throat. 'Now, if I could ask you all to study the person on the screen?'

'Who is she?' Archie wondered aloud.

'She's someone the MI6 Threat Assessment Group – or TAG for short – has identified as posing a significant threat to Toby Winchester's safety at this weekend's Student Games.'

'I thought this was just a routine surveillance detail?' Agent X-ray queried.

Highwater sucked her teeth. 'Up until twenty-four hours ago it was,' she said. 'But new information puts a different slant on things.'

Holden Grey stepped forward and tapped the TV monitor. 'The woman before you is Miss Tension. First name Evelyn.'

'But who is she?' asked Gemma, crossing her arms resolutely.

'Before I answer that,' said Highwater, 'I want you to take a careful look at these people and tell me what you think they have in common.'

The three young agents watched as a series of photographs flashed up on the monitor. The four new images were of an old lady in a rain mac, a young Chinese nurse, a teenage boy and a paunchy middle-aged businessman.

'Do they all know Evelyn Tension?' asked Archie.

'Sort of,' said Highwater.

'Are they all related to her?' Gemma wondered.

'In a way,' said Grey.

'I've got it!' Barney whooped. 'They *are* all Miss Tension.'

'Seriously, Barney!' Archie snorted. 'She can't be the same size as a teenage boy and a fifteen-stone man!'

Barney sighed with exasperation. 'Have you ever heard of a fat suit or watched *Mission Impossible*? At the beginning of the film this old Russian dude persuades a baddie to tell him the name of his big boss. Then the Russian guy pulls off his rubber mask and, boom, he's Tom Cruise.'

'Er, hello?' mocked Gemma. 'You do know that was only a movie, right? Tom Cruise is an *actor*. You see, what happens is someone makes up a story, then actors pretend to be the characters in the story and somebody else films it. The trick is that none of it is real – it's all just pretend.'

Gemma and Barney exchanged sarcastic smiles.

Highwater's voice interrupted their face-off. 'Agent X-ray, have you heard of the expression *Truth is stranger than fiction*?'

'Of course,' Gemma replied defensively.

'Never has that phrase been more appropriate than in this case,' said Highwater, raising her eyebrows. 'It appears Agent Zulu's encyclopedic knowledge of

73

fictional spy facts has given him an instinctive edge.'

'When it comes to spies Barney knows every trick in every book,' Archie added, slapping his friend on the back. 'And every trick in every movie or TV show. That's why he's such an invaluable member of STINKBOMB.'

'Oh yes, that's *right*.' Highwater clicked her fingers. 'I knew there had to be some reason he was on the team.'

'Sorry?' said Gemma, holding up both palms. 'Are you telling me that all those pictures were the same woman?'

'Yes, we believe every single person is Miss Tension,' said Highwater.

'You could ask anyone in Interpol or MI6 or the CIA,' suggested Grey. 'Very few would dispute that she is the, er, undisputed queen of disguise.'

'Who is she though?' asked Archie.

Helen Highwater drew a sheet of A4 paper from an envelope, slid on her spectacles and striding up and down in front of her audience, read out what was written on the paper.

'Evelyn Tension was educated at Marlborough College and Cambridge University, where she studied Marine Physics, before going on to earn her PhD with a paper entitled "Sustaining Human Life in Sub-Marine

Habitats". During her time in Cambridge Miss Tension was recruited by Her Majesty's Secret Services.'

'As I suspected.' Barney nodded knowingly.

'After a few years as an agent she volunteered to join MI6's elite undercover team – known as the Scalpel Unit,' said Highwater flatly. 'She passed the selection process with ease and soon she was a highly trained Scalpel. Her job was to cleanly and clinically remove or eliminate certain *parasites*.'

Barney drew in breath sharply and whispered, 'She was a Nikita.'

'What does that mean?' Gemma demanded.

'You know, like an assassin.'

'No, Agent Zulu, she was not *like* an assassin,' Highwater barked. Gemma sniggered. 'She *was* an assassin.' Gemma's amusement suddenly dispersed. 'Not only was Tension a cold-blooded, ruthless killer,' Highwater continued, 'she also taught herself to be an absolute master of disguise. Her ability to maintain her cover under the closest scrutiny meant she was MI6's number one choice for Top Secret kill-or-capture missions.'

Archie thought he could hear his own heart beating in the silence that followed Highwater's bombshell.

'Who did she k-kill?' he stammered at last.

'Bad guys.' Highwater shrugged. 'They were mostly enemy assassins but her targets varied – anyone from a Kenyan diplomat who was secretly planning a terrorist attack, to the infamous Klaus Von Grosskopf, the German robotics professor who was planning to blow up Buckingham Palace with an animatronic Corgi.'

'Couldn't these people have just been . . . arrested?' Archie asked, feeling a little sick.

'Agent Yankee,' Highwater sighed. 'Scalpel Units are only employed in exceptional circumstances – i.e. when time is too short to stop and ask questions or when dealing with individuals who operate beyond the reach of normal law enforcement channels.'

'Why do you suspect she's gone rogue?' asked Barney.

'It came to our knowledge that she was moonlighting,' explained Holden Grey. 'She was selling her services to the highest bidder.'

'You mean, she was, like, a hitman?' Gemma gasped.

'A contract killer – exactly,' Highwater said with disdain, picking some fluff off her lapel. 'She didn't care who the target was, or who wanted them killed, as long as she got paid handsomely.'

'MI6 grew suspicious when two influential Greek businessmen died in a car crash in Corfu,' Highwater said. 'At the time Evelyn Tension was on holiday – sailing round the Greek islands.'

'Why didn't you bring her in?' asked Gemma.

'We tried,' said Grey wearily. 'But she kept giving us the slip. Besides which we could never prove she was responsible. She was a highly trained professional Scalpel – it was her job to make every hit look like an accident.'

'Things came to a head by chance five years ago,' Highwater continued. 'While on a family cruise, an MI6 agent noticed a fellow passenger acting suspiciously. After monitoring the suspect our agent discovered the passenger was planning to sink the liner in the middle of the Pacific. The agent reported their discovery to HQ – just in case the saboteur was working on an undercover mission. The Secret Service had no personnel on duty on the ship so the Prime Minister ordered an intervention. The hijacker turned out to be Agent Tension. We believe she had been contracted by a foreign gangland boss to assassinate an off-duty police chief who was close to busting his drug-running cartel – something she planned to do by blowing up the whole ship.'

'But she would have killed hundreds of innocent people,' Gemma said with outrage.

'Thousands, probably,' Highwater nodded. 'Luckily our operative acted promptly. However, as the agent attempted to restrain Miss Tension a struggle broke out, during which Agent Tension was thrown overboard. A body was never recovered but we presumed she had drowned.' Highwater paused and pressed the remote control again. A document appeared on the monitor. 'Until this letter was delivered to the PM yesterday at oh-seven-hundred hours.'

Archie focused on the detail of the text, his mind subconsciously noting the pale blue cartridge paper, on which the lettering had been inscribed using blue-black ink and a fine nib.

Dear Prime Minister Winchester,

Long time no see! I expect you thought I was safely locked in a watery grave at the bottom of the ocean. I'm so sorry to disappoint you but I am alive and well – though still wounded by your betrayal. I sacrificed everything so I could defend my country, and how did you

repay me? You ordered a fellow agent to leave me for dead. Well now it's payback time, Prime Minister. I am going to take from you what you took from me – everything you hold dear. Be warned.

Much love,

Evelyn Tension

'Wow,' Barney exhaled. 'I'd say she has a few issues.'

'I'd say she's a few letters short of a cipher,' Gemma added.

'What does she mean when she says she lost everything she held dear?' Archie asked, still studying the letter.

'Members of the Scalpel Unit are forbidden from forming relationships,' Highwater explained. 'They have to cut ties with their families and friends. In a sense they operate like robots, going from mission to mission following orders, devoid of emotional attachments. They give up everything.'

'No wonder she's feeling a bit hacked off,' Archie muttered.

'What did you say, Agent Yankee?' Highwater barked.

Archie shrugged uneasily, sensing he was on shaky ground. 'I just mean it must be pretty rubbish to lose all contact with your family and have no mates. It sounds like she did a lot of the government's dirty work for years. She obviously got greedy or went crazy or something but, looking at it from her point of view, I almost . . . feel . . . sorry for her.'

'And I'm sorry you're troubled by the Secret Service's "dirty" tactics,' Highwater said in an arctic whisper, miming air quotes. She was standing in front of Archie, her nose just inches from his. 'But unfortunately the business of protecting our country is not always a pleasant one. Good people have to do bad things. That's life. One day, as a STINKBOMB agent, you may be called upon to sacrifice someone close to you in order to protect national security. I trust, when that time comes, you can be relied upon to carry out your duty?'

Archie nodded slowly, suppressing a tremor in his right leg. 'Yes, IC.'

'The Scalpel Unit's missions are extremely dangerous,' continued Highwater. 'Scalpel agents are required to operate as ruthless clinical machines. Emotional ties are a luxury they can't afford. But they are all willing volunteers who choose to join this elite black-ops unit. And thank heavens they do because the national security of our nation depends on them.'

Archie said nothing for a moment, considering what sort of person would willingly give up their family – give up everything – to protect their country. He wondered if he would be so committed if push came to shove.

After a while he said, 'So how's Tension plotting to get back at the PM?'

'Good question,' said Grey. 'Right now MI6 is pursuing several theoretical . . . theories at this time—'

'The one we're most concerned with,' Highwater interrupted, 'is the possibility that she's planning to target the Prime Minister's family. Having lost touch with her own parents when she joined the Scalpel Unit, we believe Tension may want to inflict the same ordeal on Mr Winchester.'

'Are his parents attending the competition tomorrow?' asked Gemma.

Highwater shook her head. 'The Prime Minister's parents both passed away some time ago and his wife is in Canada on an official visit, already under close guard as part of this operation. Tomorrow, as briefed, you will all be concerned with surveying and protecting the Prime Minister's son, Toby. Your orders

81

remain unchanged but this letter raises the stakes immeasurably. What was a routine operation now carries a substantial and credible threat. Does anybody have any questions?'

'Are you invoking a Level Alpha-Three protocol?' Barney enquired. 'Or are you going with tac-teams running purple ops?'

'Let me rephrase.' Highwater's eyes lingered on Barney for a moment. 'Does anybody have any *sensible* questions?'

'What exactly do you think Tension might be planning to do at the games?' Archie asked quietly.

'Worst-case scenario?' Helen Highwater removed her glasses and made eye contact with each agent in turn. 'We believe Evelyn Tension is planning to kill Toby Winchester.'

Chapter 10

Archie could hear the squishy beat of blood in his eardrums and feel it throbbing in his temples. He looked at Barney and Gemma, who both seemed as stunned as he was by Highwater's bombshell.

'So Agent Tension is a trained assassin,' he said weakly. 'Not only is she adept at dispatching dangerous criminals using numerous ingenious, yet lethal, methods *but also* she's a master of disguise so she'll be impossible to identify. And you want us to stop her bumping off Toby Winchester?'

'Precisely,' Highwater replied.

'Easy-peasy,' said Archie under his breath. 'Maybe we should do it blindfolded just to give ourselves a challenge.'

'I know it sounds daunting, Agent Yankee,' Highwater said. 'But don't forget the sports stadium will be crawling with scores of Personal Protection Officers as well as undercover MI5 and 6 agents. They'll be ready to intervene and apprehend so it's not like you'll be expected to tackle Agent Tension yourselves.

'Obviously you will monitor Toby closely but he will be accompanied by his bodyguard at all times. Even when he's in the ring, his PPO will be in his corner. Your primary job, Yankee, is to mix with the other competitors – scrutinise them up close. If Tension is planning to strike she could do so disguised as an old lady or a teenage boxer. Everyone is a suspect. If you notice anyone in that arena acting suspiciously, then you report it to me immediately. I'll be with the Mobile Surveillance Unit parked outside the venue, along with Huge Ego, I mean Hugh Figo, and a senior officer from the Metropolitan Police. We'll assimilate all intelligence from the field and coordinate the entire operation.'

'Doesn't Huge Ego want us to fall on our faces though?' Gemma demanded, planting her hands on her hips. 'He thought it was a bad idea to use kids as agents from the beginning and he can't wait for STINKBOMB to fail so he can say *I told you so.*'

Helen Highwater hesitated. In truth she shared Agent X-ray's mistrust of her boss but she was obliged to follow operational protocol and Hugh Figo was her immediate superior. 'I think Mr Figo views STINKBOMB in an altogether more positive light after your successful inaugural mission,' she said, managing a reassuring smile. 'And, if we fail to protect Toby Winchester tomorrow, Figo's neck will be on the line just as much as ours.'

Archie nodded as he digested the news in silence. The stakes couldn't be much higher for their second mission. 'I feel sick,' he whispered.

'Me too,' Barney agreed – his words strangely garbled. Archie turned and saw that his friend was feeding the last two inches of a Snickers bar into his already overstuffed mouth.

'No wonder *you* feel sick!' Archie smirked.

Barney shrugged, pushing the chocolate to the inside of his cheek, like a giant hamster. 'The only way to deal with nausea is to feed it,' he explained, flicking his balled-up wrapper into Archie's face.

'That's enough joking around,' Highwater barked. 'I understand you're all excited and anxious about Operation Gumshield but it is of utmost importance that you pay attention to Mr Grey for the next few minutes. He's about to brief you on the equipment you'll be allocated.'

'Follow me, agents.' Holden Grey strode to the workshop at the far end of the room and positioned himself behind the long wooden bench.

'Here come the gadgets,' Barney whispered excitedly.

Holden Grey placed three slender black mobile phones on the bench. Archie, Barney and Gemma exchanged looks of concern.

'Er, I don't want to spoil the party,' said Gemma, 'but we've all seen an iPhone before.'

'I'm sure you have, Agent X-ray.' Holden Grey's pencil-thin moustache twitched as he stifled his grin. 'But these are not iPhones. I have personally myself made certain modifications to the factory fit on these particular devices. What you are looking at is what I like to call the *spiPhone*.'

Holden Grey picked up one of the phones and switched it on. A ripple of intrigue animated the three agents.

'I have implanted a tiny radio transmitter into each device that will transmit on a dedicated FM frequency,' explained Grey. 'This will allow IC and the surveillance

86

team to monitor the position of your exact locations at all times during the operation. Also, in addition, you will be able to stay in touch with each other by using the transmitter in conjunction with these standard issue two-way earpieces. And, finally, I have adapted the spiPhone's camera by fitting its flash with an ultra-high-frequency particle oscillator.'

'Un-believable,' Barney cooed. Then his wide eyes narrowed. 'What does that mean?'

Grey smiled kindly. 'When it's enabled, this function vibrates the molecules in whatever solid object the camera is pointed at. Within a few nanoseconds all the particles will be aligned and oscillating in time.' The old man watched his audience expectantly.

'Then what, Mr Grey?' Gemma asked, turning her palms upward.

'Imagine the molecules are a pile of spaghetti,' Grey suggested. 'When they are all tangled up they make a great solid mass obliterating the plate, right? But what if they were all straightened out and spaced at regular intervals?'

'You'd be able to see the plate?' Archie suggested with a note of disbelief.

'Clever boy!' Holden Grey snapped his fingers.

'Are you saying that with the spiPhone we will be able to see through solid objects?'

'Not with the naked eye, young man,' Grey said. 'Even though the spaghetti is lined up it's still vibrating at an incredibly high frequency. But if you were to take a snapshot at any time, with say a high-speed camera –' he tapped the handset he was holding – 'then you would be able to see through the object.'

Archie shook his head slowly in awe while Barney's eyes were bulging and his mouth hung slightly open so it was left to Gemma to speak. 'So you've, like, invented an actual X-ray camera?'

Holden Grey puffed out his chest and smiled. 'Correct.'

'So we can point it at walls and stuff and it'll take a picture of what's on the other side?' asked Archie, still shaking his head in awe.

Grey pursed his lips. 'Not exactly. I haven't quite perfected the beam,' he confessed. 'There are still some materials that remain impervious to the effects of the high-frequency particle oscillator.'

'When you say *some materials* . . .' Archie prompted. 'Which ones do you mean?'

'Oh let me think . . . the camera can't see through

88

brick for a start. Nor cement, stone, plasterboard, or wood. And it can't see through metals. It also can't see through fibreglass, enamel, plastic, natural or man-made fabrics, earth, sand, slate, marble, leather, fur or any fluids.'

Sensing the enormous disappointment in the room, Archie frantically searched his mind for a substance Grey hadn't included on his list. 'You didn't mention rubber,' he offered brightly. 'So the particle vibrating thingy isn't completely powerless on rubber?'

'Heavens no!' Grey said dismissively. 'In fact quite the reverse.'

'What does that mean, exactly?' pressed Gemma.

'Interestingly the atomic bonds within some rubber composites are precisely eighty picometres which is exactly the right length to resonate perfectly with the HFO beam.' Holden Grey raised his eyebrows as if hearing this surprising fact for the first time himself. 'If exposed to the beam for even a split second the bonds disintegrate completely.'

'So what happens to the rubber?' Barney asked.

'Ppfff.' Holden Grey spread the fingers on one hand. 'It melts. Then it's vaporised into, well, vapour.'

'So the HFO beam is useless against most solid

objects,' Barney surmised dejectedly. 'And it vaporises some rubber polymers in seconds. Are there any substances it can actually see through?'

'Of course,' Grey replied positively.

'Which ones?' Barney said eagerly.

Holden Grey cleared his throat. 'Glass.'

'Glass!?' the three agents chorused.

Holden Grey nodded apologetically. 'Provided it's not smoked or pebbled.'

Archie smiled warmly at the old man. 'So, is it fair to say that the only material the X-ray camera can see through . . . is see-through already?'

Holden Grey looked thoughtfully at his invention for a moment. 'I suppose so, yes,' he said with a slight laugh. 'I hadn't really thought about it like that.'

During the long uncomfortable silence that followed, even Archie couldn't think of anything positive to say.

'OK, STINKBOMB,' Highwater announced, breaking the silence. 'I think we're all up to speed now on the various shortcomings of the spiPhone's X-ray camera function. As Mr Grey mentioned it is a work in progress and I'm sure there'll be a software upgrade to download sooner or later.' She forced her lips into the briefest smile before continuing. 'Anyway, time is short so let's draw a line under that for the time being.'

Archie nodded, thinking it might be better just to draw a line through it.

'Do you have anything else for us, Mr Grey?' asked Barney with a hint of desperation.

'Oh yes, I almost forgot!' Holden Grey's eyes popped open and he held up one finger. Patting himself down he reached inside his hooded sweatshirt and produced a slender black ballpoint pen, which he handed to Barney.

'OK.' Barney nodded, his full cheeks colouring again. 'I'm not going to make the same mistake as last time. This isn't a gadget, is it? It's just a normal pen, and you want us to sign for the spiPhones, right?'

Holden Grey smiled kindly. 'Wrong,' he said. 'You are holding a magno-pen – a stun-gun capable of immobilising any human, animal or indeed electronic equipment within a ten-metre range for thirty seconds. It's based on a classic MI6 gadget that was commonly issued to spies during the Cold War. You simply twist the pen barrel to arm the device, then when you click the button to extend the ballpoint, the electric charge starts building. A second click retracts the nib which then dispenses the charge at the target. It's very accurate and very powerful.'

91

'So you just twist and click twice?' Barney asked mischievously, turning the pen's barrel and pointing it at Gemma.

'You dare, Zulu,' she warned.

'I wouldn't do that if I were you, Agent Zulu,' Grey advised. 'Operating the weapon is not quite that simple.'

Barney wasn't listening. With a wicked grin on his face he clicked the button on the end of the pen to extend its nib.

'Seriously, Barney. I'm warning you!' Gemma threatened.

Barney savoured the look of dread on her face for a moment, then spun and, aiming the pen at a digital alarm clock on a table behind Holden Grey, retracted its point.

There was a loud crack like a bullwhip, and a flash.

Archie was staring expectantly at the digital clock when he heard a dull thud that sounded like someone had dropped a sack of potatoes on to the floor right next to him. Turning sharply and looking down he saw Barney spreadeagled on the floor, his mouth lolling open and his eyes staring blankly at the ceiling.

'Barney!' he yelped, dropping to his friend's aid.

'Don't worry, Archie,' Holden Grey said reassuringly.

'He's just stunned. He'll be fine in about thirty seconds.'

Gemma dragged over a plastic chair and Archie grabbed Barney under his armpits, pulling his friend to his feet and dumping him into the seat.

Everyone watched anxiously for a while until Barney blinked hard a couple of times and opened his eyes.

'What happened?' he slurred groggily, scratching his hair, which was standing on end, crackling with static.

'I think your little joke backfired,' Gemma said drily.

'I – I don't get it,' Barney said sleepily. 'I just wanted to take out the clock. I followed the instructions. Twist, click, click. Simple.'

'Not *quite*,' Holden Grey countered. 'With this model you must wait ten seconds between clicks to allow time for the electric charge within the pen to build. Otherwise . . .'

'The pen itself is electrified,' Barney said sheepishly. 'And whoever's holding it gets the shock of their life.'

'Hold on,' Gemma protested. 'How come our pens don't work like the originals?'

Holden Grey wagged the pen gently between his thumb and forefinger. 'The electromagnetic components in these pens are highly specialised parts that are incredibly difficult and expensive to manufacture.

93

It would certainly prove well beyond STINKBOMB's limited resources to finance such equipment.'

'So where did that one come from?' Gemma asked, nodding at the pen as Grey dropped it into a plastic bag.

Grey smiled. 'The magno-pens you will be issued with have all been salvaged from the MI6 Decommissioned Field Equipment Storage Facility. Aka and also known as the scrapheap.'

'So our pens are duds?' Gemma protested. 'You're issuing us with broken stuff?'

'Not really,' Highwater explained. 'Mr Grey has found a brilliant way of re-energising the old magno-pens to enable them to generate one more electromagnetic shock. You just need to know how to use it safely. I'm sure you'll agree the weapon will provide you with an invaluable means of protection if you find yourself in close quarters with Miss Tension.'

Great, Archie thought. I suppose we just ask her nicely if she wouldn't mind not killing us for ten seconds while we charge up our secret weapon.

'Does anyone have any questions?' Highwater asked.

Barney's hand shot up.

'Nobody?' Highwater asked.

'I have one,' Barney called out.

94

'Good,' Highwater said conclusively. 'In that case let's run through everyone's responsibilities for tomorrow's mission.'

For the next two hours Highwater briefed the team on the layout of the venue for the Student Games, drilled them again on their cover stories and ran through the MI6 files on Evelyn Tension one more time.

'Finally, here are your passwords and go codes for the operation,' Highwater said, handing each child an A4 folder. 'Agent X-ray has devised the terminology which you will all have committed to memory by the morning. Shred the documents when you have done so. Agent X-ray will spend the night here in the safe house with Mr Grey and me. Tomorrow morning at oh-seven-hundred hours, sharp, Agents X-ray, Yankee and Zulu will rendezvous at Number One, Clifftops.'

'That's my house,' Archie said, surprised.

'Well then, Agent Yankee.' Highwater smiled. 'You've got no excuse for being late, have you? You will all be met by Mr Richard Hunt who will brief you on the modifications that have been made to the transportation solution he has kindly donated to STINKBOMB.'

'Transportation solution?' Archie repeated.

Highwater nodded. 'A brand new customised plane

designed specially for STINKBOMB's use on secret missions – the Dragonfly X.'

'Archie's dad's given us an aeroplane?' Gemma said. 'Wicked!'

'Is my dad flying us to London?' Archie asked, beaming.

Helen Highwater shook her head. 'No, Archie. The Dragonfly X is an official STINKBOMB vehicle and, as such, only official STINKBOMB agents are authorised to operate it.'

Archie felt a buzz of excitement at the prospect of flying the Dragonfly solo again. Since STINKBOMB's first mission, when he'd proved his skill as a pilot, his father had given him intensive training in flying the Dragonfly – concentrating on hovering, high performance manoeuvres and low-level flying. Although his father had given him plenty of praise, he'd never suggested that Archie should fly the plane solo. And he hadn't so much as hinted at his intentions to donate a customised Dragonfly to MI6.

No matter how dangerous the flying training he'd done over recent months, Archie had always known that his father could take the stick if things started getting difficult. Knowing he was going to be in sole control of

96

the aircraft again was both thrilling and terrifying.

'Your father has been reporting to us after each of your training flights,' Highwater said. 'He thinks you're ready.'

Archie smiled proudly.

'Briefing over,' Highwater announced. 'Mr Grey and I will travel to the sports stadium by car. We will all RV at the south-east car park of the arena at oh-nine-hundred hours for a final mission brief before going undercover. Get a good night's sleep, everyone.'

Chapter 11

It was five past seven on Saturday morning – still an hour before dawn. Archie had slept badly, unable to switch his mind off from thinking about today's mission – Operation Gumshield. Nervous but excited he strode wearily with his dad towards the private hangar in the grounds at the rear of their house. Thick frost coated the grass and trees and the cloudless black sky was peppered with tiny dots of brilliant light. Spotlights along the edge of the path highlighted the dense white plumes that billowed out of his mouth as his warm breath mixed with the sub-zero air of the early winter morning.

'I can't believe you never told me you were customising a Dragonfly for STINKBOMB,' Archie enthused, still on a high after hearing he'd be flying solo again.

'You're not the only one who can be secretive round here.' Archie's father smiled to himself. 'The Dragonfly X only came out of the factory yesterday – I picked it up while you were at school.'

'So what modifications does it have?'

'You'll know everything in a few minutes.'

Barney and Gemma, who had been following a few paces behind, broke into a jog to catch up with Archie and his father.

'Does it have a button that converts it into a submarine?' Barney asked eagerly.

'I'm afraid not, Barney.' Richard Hunt laughed.

'What about weapons?' Barney suggested excitedly. 'It could have a ray-gun that cuts through steel, or a smart bomb that takes out any vehicle within a three-mile radius.'

'It could . . .' Richard Hunt said mysteriously, '. . . but it doesn't.'

The four figures cut across a wide lawn and headed into a bank of densely planted fir trees. Beyond the copse was a large grass quadrangle about half the size of a football pitch, hemmed on all sides by a thick wall of firs. They marched across the secluded field and stopped in front of a large metal structure with double doors and a shallow pitched roof.

'Maybe it has some sort of invisibility cloak?' Barney said, his chubby cheeks almost glowing in the cold.

'Er, you're thinking of *Harry Potter*,' Gemma offered, her voice muffled by the black and white desert scarf she'd pulled up over her mouth.

'I meant like an electronic cloaking device,' Barney countered. 'Not an *actual* cloak. That would be crazy.'

'You're right,' Gemma nodded. '*I'm* the crazy one.'

'To be fair, Barney's predictions have been more accurate than ours,' Archie pointed out.

'How about supersonic rocket boosters?' Barney turned to Richard Hunt. 'Or anti-aircraft-missile jamming lasers? Oooh, I know – you could have redesigned the fuselage so it floats and given it retractable wings to convert it into a speedboat.'

'It's not the Batplane,' Gemma laughed.

'Actually Barney's on the right lines,' Archie's father announced.

'Told you so,' Archie whispered to Gemma.

'But instead of playing this guessing game for another half-hour,' Richard Hunt continued, 'fun as it

100

is, how about we go inside the hangar and take a look?'

He produced a small silver key fob from his pocket and pressed one of its buttons. A motor purred into life and the hangar's double doors slid open, their well-oiled wheels trundling smoothly on their runners. Richard Hunt stepped into the building and flicked a couple of switches on the wall inside.

'OK, guys,' he said, as the fluorescent tubes overhead buzzed and flickered. 'This is the Dragonfly X.'

At that moment the hangar was lit up with a steady hum and Archie, Barney and Gemma stared silently at the jet plane housed within. The Dragonfly X shared the same basic features as the previous Mark 600, plane. It had a sleek torpedo-shaped nose and the familiar swept wings, each underslung with a vectored-thrust jet engine. Archie thought the glass dome encompassing the four-seater cockpit was more streamlined than before and the slight upturn of the plane's wingtips seemed more pronounced. But the most striking difference was that the Dragonfly X was not silver as its predecessors had been – it was rendered altogether more rugged and imposing by being painted all over in matt black.

'It's awesome,' Archie said, running his hand over its curves.

101

'OMG, Mr Hunt,' Gemma enthused. 'It's totally fly.'

'Why the new colour scheme, Mr Hunt?' Barney asked, frowning and scratching his chin. 'I'm assuming the paint contains grains of H_2C_3PO or some other compound designed to diffract enemy radar?'

'No,' Richard Hunt shrugged. 'We just thought it looked cool. Although our designers predict the slight roughness of the skin will improve boundary layer adhesion resulting in a reduced fuel burn of about two per cent.'

'Obviously,' Barney agreed with a nod. 'It's simple aerodynamics, isn't it?'

'You'll be pleased to know we've done a little more than just tweak the plane's profile and give it a mean paintjob. Follow me.' Richard Hunt circled the aircraft slowly, ducking underneath the aircraft's wing and patting its belly.

'The Dragonfly X is fitted with an auxiliary fuel tank that increases its endurance by sixty per cent so you could easily drop in on an evil genius two thousand miles away. At the same time the engines now produce an extra ten per cent of thrust so your take-off performance won't be hindered by the weight of the extra fuel.' Slapping one of the plane's tyres he added, 'Plus we've strengthened the undercarriage ready for any rugged terrain you might want to land on.' Completing his circuit of the plane, Archie's father paused and placed his hand on its rear fuselage. 'As per the Mark 600, the X comes with desert, urban and woodland camouflage nets as standard.'

'Ahh,' Gemma whispered into Barney's ear. 'Those must be the invisibility cloaks you were going on about?'

Richard Hunt placed a foot in the small recess just below the glass canopy and pulled himself up on to the outside of the Dragonfly. Unlatching the dome he slid it back and climbed into the right-hand front seat. 'Hop in,' he said. Barney and Gemma climbed into the cockpit's two back seats while Archie climbed into the left-hand front seat. Immediately he noticed a switch on the front instrument panel that he'd never seen before. Next to the lever used to raise and lower the Dragonfly's landing gear was a small red toggle.

'What's that for?' he asked eagerly.

'That operates the ATLAS.'

'ATLAS?' Archie echoed.

His father nodded. 'The Aquatic Terrain Landing Assistance System,' he said, touching the toggle. 'If you flick the ATLAS switch down before lowering the undercarriage, your wheels won't come down.'

'How come?'

'Instead, two canoe-shaped floats will be lowered from the undercarriage bay on hydraulic struts.'

'You mean the Dragonfly X can be used as a float plane?' Archie asked, grinning.

'Three-quarters of the world's surface is covered by sea,' his father replied. 'It stands to reason you may be forced to land on it sooner or later.' He turned and pointed past the back seats to a hatch in the rear bulkhead. 'In there is your sea survival equipment – sea anchor, life raft, desalination packets . . .'

'Chocolate?' Barney suggested.

Richard Hunt smiled. 'Oh don't worry, Barney, there's plenty of chocolate in there. Plus three sets of scuba gear in case you have to swim to safety undercover. I understand you've all completed the MI6 Deep Water Survival course?'

The three agents nodded. Archie smiled wryly, remembering the ribbing he'd been given by Harvey Newman, who'd overheard him talking to Barney about their weekend swimming lessons.

Hey everyone – Hunt and Jones are having extra swimming lessons, Newman had scoffed. *What a couple of wusses.*

Archie had endured days of ridicule from most of his

classmates and someone (probably Harvey Newman) had placed a child's rubber ring on his chair every morning for weeks.

Of course, Archie never mentioned that he'd actually been undergoing an intensive Scuba course and underwater combat training with experienced Special Boat Service (SBS) commandos.

Richard Hunt turned to address Gemma. 'As you're the computer whizz in the team you'll be most interested to know that Dragonfly X is equipped with a full Mode F comms kit.'

'Mode Foxtrot!' Barney exclaimed. 'That's so cool.'

Gemma fixed Barney with a heavy-lidded gaze. 'Do you even know what a Mode F comms kit is, Zulu?'

'Yeah,' Barney replied cockily. 'Pretty much. More or less.'

'Do you or not?'

Barney puffed out his cheeks. 'Nope.'

'It's a dedicated network offering two way communication with any MI6-controlled station, including classified databases and satellites,' lectured Gemma.

'So I was right.' Barney smiled nervously. 'That is *so* cool.'

Richard Hunt tapped one of the screens on the instrument panel in front of him. 'This is normally the co-pilot's navigation display but it easily converts into the Mode F interface.' Archie's father pushed a square black button on the overhead panel and a slim computer keyboard slid out from under the screen, which flicked from its normal map display to show a long list of different options. Halfway down the screen Archie noticed the words 'Access Satellite Control Menu'.

'Whoa!' he grinned. 'Don't tell me we can actually control satellites with this thing?'

'Of course you can't.' Gemma patted him on the shoulder. 'But *I* definitely can.'

'That's amazing,' Archie said.

'I won't let it go to my head,' Gemma smiled.

'Not you. I meant the comms kit.'

'I think we all know what you meant,' Gemma replied, inspecting her deep purple nail polish.

Archie pretended to study one of the plane's switches, his cheeks burning.

'OK,' Richard Hunt interjected. 'You're all up to speed with the new features so I'd better let you get to wherever it is you're going.'

Archie felt sudden panic sucking at his insides as

he watched his father clamber out of the plane. Last time he'd flown the Dragonfly solo he'd been so fired up with adrenalin he hadn't stopped to consider the responsibility he was taking on. As he watched his father walk round the front of the aircraft a voice in his head was saying, 'You can't fly this without him. You need him in case things go wrong. Twelve-year-olds can't fly jet planes, you wally. Twelve-year-olds build Lego and play football.'

Archie's father approached the aircraft next to Archie's seat.

'Your route's already loaded into the nav box,' he said. 'MI6 sent it through remotely this morning. Just type in your mission password and away you go.'

Feeling strangely sick, Archie nodded. He tried to smile but he seemed to have lost control of his face. His father took a step closer, stepped into the foothold in the fuselage and pulled himself up.

'I almost forgot,' he said, leaning into the cockpit. 'Down here in your footwell is the auxiliary fuel-tank shut-off valve.'

Archie leaned over and peered at his feet, so that his head almost touched his father's.

'Believe in yourself, Archie. You can do this,' Richard

Hunt whispered. 'I wouldn't let you go if I didn't think you could hack it.'

Archie gave his father a single nod.

'Take care, kiddo.' Richard winked and lowered himself to the floor. 'Good luck, STINKBOMB,' he added as he walked out of the hangar.

Archie took a deep breath, willing himself to take his dad's advice. He stared at the array of buttons and switches on the instrument panels around him – all of which looked strangely baffling.

'Come on then, ace. Let's hit the sky.'

Archie turned to see that Gemma had jumped into the front seat next to his. Her crooked fringe was masking one eye but the other was twinkling and she was actually smiling.

Archie nodded and reached over his head to slide the canopy shut. 'Let's do this,' he said as confidently as he could.

Within a minute he had run through his pre-take-off checks and the Dragonfly's two jet engines were whining eagerly. He released the parking brake and the plane rolled out of the hangar on to the grass outside. Stopping in the middle of the field Archie pulled the nozzle lever to the hover stop and the engines' nozzles swivelled until they were directing their thrust straight downward. Archie took another deep breath.

'Everyone ready?' he asked.

'You bet,' said Gemma.

'That's a roger, over,' replied Barney.

'OK then. Let's go.' Archie swallowed hard – then he slammed the thrust levers forward and the plane's engines began to roar. 'Look out, London, here we come.'

Chapter 12

The Dragonfly soared into the air, powering vertically towards the stars.

'I'd forgotten how wicked this thing is. It's like being in a lift,' Gemma marvelled, watching the square field shrinking below her.

Archie gently worked the Dragonfly's controls, coordinating small movements of the joystick and the rudder pedals. He suddenly realised that his nerves had vanished. He could feel what the plane was doing in the tips of his fingers and toes and he instinctively knew how to control it. Archie flicked the gear lever to the up position, retracting the plane's undercarriage, then slid the nozzle lever fully forward. As the engine nozzles rotated they directed their hot exhaust gas rearwards, accelerating the aircraft forward at a terrific rate and forcing its three occupants back in their seats.

'Nice work, Agent Yankee,' Gemma chuckled.

Archie couldn't help smiling to himself as he eased the stick back and the Dragonfly's nose climbed eastward, towards the gently glowing horizon.

'So what's the mission password?' asked Archie, his hand poised over the flight computer's keypad.

'You're supposed to have learned all the mission protocols by now,' Gemma replied, looking smug.

'Boys are rubbish,' Barney piped up from the back seat.

'Sorry, Agent Zulu?' said Gemma. 'I didn't quite catch that.'

'I said, "Boys are rubbish,"' Barney said obligingly. 'I'm pretty sure that's right. Yeah. Definitely. Boys are rubbish.'

'Thank you, Agent Zulu,' smiled Gemma. 'I couldn't have put it better myself.'

With a weary sigh Archie typed the words *Boys are rubbish* into the computer and a list of radio beacons instantly appeared on the screen. Clicking the transmit switch he spoke into the microphone on his headset.

'London control, this is Sulphur One, reaching six thousand feet heading east. Request further climb and airways clearance.'

'Sulphur One, this is London control. Climb to flight level one-five-zero and route to Southampton VOR.'

Archie repeated his instructions and banked to the left.

'So are all our passwords and codes for this mission going to be about girls being better than boys?' he enquired.

Gemma stared at the orange sun rapidly emerging from behind the horizon as the aircraft rocketed higher and higher. 'The passwords are set in stone,' she said. 'I'm not authorised to change them.'

'What about codes for secret communication between agents?' Barney suggested. 'I noticed you don't have any of those in place yet. What if I needed a secret code to warn another agent to hit the deck.'

'Right,' Gemma said warily. 'I guess IC didn't think that was a situation we're likely to face during Gumshield. She just briefed me on more general stuff like "Girls rule", which means *All agents report to the rendezvous point.*'

'Sure,' Barney agreed. 'But imagine one of us has discovered that Evelyn Tension is about to detonate some sort of device that sends out a pulse at waist

112

height and takes out everything in its path?'

'That's a good point,' Gemma teased. 'I can't believe we haven't agreed a protocol for such a regular, everyday situation.'

'Actually I don't think it's a bad idea,' said Archie. 'Having a signal for other agents to take immediate cover sounds pretty sensible to me.'

Gemma was thoughtful for a moment, then, 'Have it your way,' she said grudgingly.

Barney leaned forward so that his head was between Archie and Gemma's shoulders. 'So, how should we warn our fellow agents and make sure they get down low?'

'How about something fiendishly simple?' suggested Gemma. 'Like, oh I don't know, "Get down"?'

Barney shook his head dismissively. 'It *has* to be coded otherwise Miss Tension will realise we're taking evasive action and alter the angle of sweep of her weapon's deadly pulse.'

'I see.' Archie raised his eyebrows and pushed his glasses up his nose. 'I didn't realise this type of imaginary weapon has an adjustable sweep angle.'

'This one does,' Barney stated categorically. 'I'm thinking we could use the code "I'm having a blast".'

'Nice one,' Archie said. 'What do you think, Agent X-ray?'

'Yeah, wicked, whatever.' Gemma rolled her eyes.

Sixty miles from their destination Archie throttled back the Dragonfly's engines to idle and lowered its nose to start the descent towards the O2 Arena. Banking hard to his left he flew north for a couple of miles, putting power back on to fly level at five hundred feet over the river Thames and following its snaking course towards the city centre.

Archie caught glimpses of Big Ben and Buckingham Palace as they whipped past but he was concentrating on his flying too much to enjoy the view. At such a low level and travelling at over two hundred knots, a split second's inattention could result in the plane crashing into the water.

Gently easing the control column from side to side, Archie followed the river's fluid sweeps and watched countless landmark bridges flash just beneath him. As he rounded the distinctive horseshoe of water that cradles London's Docklands, his destination emerged from behind the mirrored faces of the Canary Wharf skyscrapers.

The O2 Arena looked like a UFO that had landed on the river's south bank, twelve bright yellow stanchions

114

protruding from the giant saucer, like alien antennae. Archie carved a right-hand turn round the circular structure and headed towards his designated helipad. He pulled the nozzle lever fully aft and the Dragonfly's forward momentum died, leaving it in a slow vertical descent. The plane settled gently on to the tarmac surface next to a normal helicopter and another privately owned Dragonfly.

'Very smooth,' Gemma marvelled. '*Someone's* been practising.'

Blushing, Archie slid the canopy back. 'My dad's a good teacher,' he muttered, looking away quicky.

'All stations from Zulu,' Barney muttered, touching an imaginary earpiece. 'Contact, Hansel and Gretel. Nine o'clock, closing fast.'

Archie looked to his left and smiled when he saw Helen Highwater and Holden Grey approaching. They were both dressed in bright yellow jackets and black trousers – the uniform of the competition's officials. To a casual observer they looked like two stewards greeting some more VIP passengers arriving in a private jet.

The three agents clambered out of the cockpit and jumped to the ground, forming a line as their superiors arrived.

'Good morning, agents,' Highwater said curtly.

'Word up,' Grey offered, bumping fists with each kid in turn.

'OK, X-ray,' Highwater continued, getting straight down to business. 'You are to report to the medical centre at the east entrance immediately. Yankee, you need to go to the competitors' registration desks in zone eleven. As briefed, the records show that you came just outside the top sixteen boxers in the qualification process so you are here purely as a reserve and won't actually be competing.'

Archie signalled his understanding with a single nod.

'Which leaves me with Agent Zulu.' Highwater peered at Barney over her glasses. 'Last but by no means . . . smallest.'

'Thank you,' Barney replied keenly.

'Mr Grey has your fake press pass and camera. Just remember, say nothing and photograph everything. Understand?'

Barney nodded and then muttered, 'The cobra is about to enter Aladdin's cave.'

'What are you wittering on about?' Highwater snapped.

'Nothing,' Barney replied, widening his eyes innocently.

'OK, guys,' Grey enthused. 'Let's bring it up.'

'I'm pretty sure he meant *bring it on*,' Gemma whispered to Archie as they headed for the arena's main entrance.

'I don't know,' Archie muttered. 'I am feeling pretty nauseous right now.'

Barney followed a few paces behind them, peering anxiously into the distance and mumbling into his sleeve, 'Zulu to Tac Team Bravo Seven – the hamsters are going underground. Operation Gumshield is live.'

As the agents receded Holden Grey called after them, 'Remember, team – stay on comms at all times. Keep talking to each other. The biggest enemy of an undercover agent is isolation. Well, apart from violent criminals I suppose. Especially trained assassins. Not to mention their evil henchmen of course – they can be vicious too. So what I'm trying to say is be careful. And if you can't be careful then the next best thing—'

'They can't hear you,' Highwater said flatly.

Holden Grey pursed his lips and stroked his thin moustache. 'You're probably right,' he said softly. 'I just worry about them so.'

'I know,' Highwater replied, adding under her breath, 'So do I . . . So do I.'

Chapter 13

As Archie, Barney and Gemma approached the main entrance to the arena, a burly man wearing an olive green parka stepped across their path and began taking photos of the agents, backing away from them as they advanced.

'All right, kids?' he called from behind his long lens. 'I'm from the local paper. Who do you reckon's going to win the boxing?'

'No comment,' Archie replied with a tight smile.

'Have you heard Toby Winchester's due to compete today?' the journalist persisted.

'Seriously,' Gemma said sternly. 'No comment.'

'What about my fellow photographer?' The man aimed his camera at Barney. 'Surely you've got an opinion on the PM's son?'

Barney shook his head vigorously and mumbled, 'No comment.'

The journalist lowered his camera and let the three agents past. As soon as they'd entered the arena they inserted their earpieces and split up. Barney turned left while Gemma turned right and Archie carried on, straight towards the middle of the dome.

As he entered the central theatre Archie turned on the spot and gazed all around. He felt dwarfed by the colossal stadium with its banks of seats sweeping round the rectangular floor space and reaching way up to the domed ceiling. The stands were almost deserted now but he tried to imagine them crammed with thousands of fans screaming for the superstars who had played here in the past, like Beyoncé or Coldplay. At those concerts the floor would have been a sweaty mass of bodies jostling and dancing to their idols' music, but today it was covered with crash mats. Four martial-arts squares were marked out on the padded floor with white tape and at the far end of the area stood two boxing rings side by side.

Archie strode past scores of officials, busily measuring competition areas and setting out umpires' chairs, and

119

joined a line of boys waiting in front of a desk that was signposted 'Boxers' Registration'.

The boy in front of Archie turned and peered at him from under the hood of his Lonsdale sweatshirt.

'Hello,' Archie said with a grin.

The boy gave Archie a confused snarl.

'How's it going?' Archie asked brightly.

The boy said nothing but acknowledged Archie with a short upward jerk of his chin, then turned away. Another boxer joined the line. Archie turned and jerked his chin at the boy, who did the same back.

OK, Archie thought. I can do this.

When he got to the front of the line he chin-jerked the woman sitting behind the desk.

'Hello, young man,' she said with a kind smile. 'What's your name?'

'Ar—' Archie stopped himself giving his real name just in time. 'Danny Hook,' he said. He couldn't believe he'd almost blown his cover at the first hurdle and his heart was drumming.

The lady gave him a curious frown before studying the paperwork in front of her. 'Ah, yes. Here you are, Danny,' she said, tapping the list of names. 'I see you're down as a reserve.'

120

Archie tried to look disappointed. 'What are my chances of boxing today, d'you reckon?'

'You never know,' the lady said brightly. 'Even if you don't get to box, it'll be a great experience.'

'I know. I don't want to miss a thing.'

After registering, Archie had a pre-fight medical with the match doctor – a tall, portly man in a tweed three-piece suit. Then a dentist checked his teeth and his gumshield before a man called Ivan showed him to the boxers' changing room.

Archie guessed Ivan was an ex-boxer by his swollen brow and his flat nose.

Nobody spoke in the changing room. Some boys were sitting on benches listening to their iPods while others were limbering up, stretching or shadow boxing. Archie gave a couple of boys the chin-jerk as he entered and found a space on the bench to park himself. Ivan told him he was to remain in the changing rooms or in the competitors' designated ringside area just in case he would be required to box, adding with a snort, 'But you've probably got more chance of winning the lottery.'

Archie changed into his boxing kit and pulled his tracksuit back on over the top. Nervously he laced up

121

his boots and wrapped his hands in crepe bandages – as all boxers do to protect their knuckles under their gloves. Although he had no intention of getting into the ring it was important to look like he knew what he was doing.

There was still an hour to go before the boxing programme was due to start so Archie decided to take a stroll. Discreetly replacing his earpiece, which he'd taken out before his medical, he left the changing room and walked towards the arena. Although it was far from full, there suddenly seemed to be a buzz inside the stadium. The first ten rows of seats were lined with spectators, some waving flags and banners in support of the athletes already competing on the judo and karate mats. A lanky-looking kid landed a match-winning kick on his opponent and a loud cheer erupted from the crowd and echoed around the cavernous hall.

'This is Yankee,' Archie whispered. 'Where are you guys?'

'North-east corner of the floor.' It was Gemma's voice. 'All quiet.'

Archie glanced instinctively to Gemma's location and saw her kneeling by a stretcher at the edge of the crash mats. She was dressed in navy blue trousers, a white shirt with black epaulettes and a navy beret.

'I'm loving the costume,' Archie muttered. 'Especially the hat. It's very . . . French.'

'Shut it. Or you might be needing this stretcher.'

Archie smirked at Gemma's response and scanned the hall. 'What's your position, Zulu?'

'I'm in deep, over,' came Barney's eager response. 'I'm blending in, in the western press enclosure.'

Archie turned to scan the photographers crouching in front of the first row of seats. All of them were hunched over their tripods, following the sporting action through their long lenses – except for one, who was standing up. And smiling and waving.

'Yeah,' Archie muttered. 'I think I see you. Are you next to the clown who's standing up and waving like a lunatic?'

'No!' Barney replied with delight. 'That actually *is* me! Look.'

With the sort of flourish normally used by magicians producing rabbits from nowhere, Barney pulled off his beanie hat to reveal his tight blond curls.

'Wow,' Archie said drily. 'So it is. I'd never have spotted you.'

There were a considerable number of uniformed

police officers peppered around the edge of the arena and he knew from the briefing that at least as many again were hidden from view. Out of sight, high in the rafters of the stadium, scores of police marksmen were watching proceedings through the telescopic sights of their high-power rifles. He knew as well that two of the vans in the car park emblazoned with the logos of news agencies contained SWAT teams, ready to storm the building at a second's notice.

But, even knowing there was such a high level of security present, Archie felt strangely vulnerable. How could they hope to identify one lone lunatic among the masses of spectators and competitors – especially one who could change her appearance at the drop of a hat? The teenage boy wearing the Chelsea shirt in the front row could easily be her, as could the man in the hat or the old lady drinking tea from a flask.

'Where are you?' Archie said under his breath. 'And what exactly is your evil intention, Evelyn Tension?'

In a

Small Room

Somewhere

in the

O2 Arena . . .

Chapter 14

Evelyn Tension studied the small digital screen on the back of the camera, nodding approvingly as she scrolled through the photographs. 'My, my, Kurt,' she whispered. 'You have been a busy boy.'

Shrugging off an olive green coat, Kurt peeled away his wig and smiled. 'And I got voice samples for all of them,' he announced proudly.

'You are an angel.' Tension batted her long eyelashes. 'I have to admit I'd rather underestimated you. If you carry on like this I may have to reconsider who is my favourite Von Grosskopf brother.'

'What's that supposed to mean?' snapped Klaus Von Grosskopf, who was wearing a tweed suit and studying a laptop computer on the other side of the small room.

127

'Do calm down, Klausy,' Tension giggled, walking her fingers up Kurt's arm. 'I'm just saying that Kurt here has surprised me with his ingenuity.'

Kurt peeled back his mask, which stretched like a rubber band before snapping free from his face and hanging limply in his hand. Tension looked at his mangled features and shuddered, her hand recoiling as if she'd touched a deadly snake.

'Goodness me, what a difference!' she exclaimed. 'Those masks are so convincing even *I'd* forgotten how repulsive you really are, Kurt.'

Kurt grinned and sniffed a slimy yellow trail of snot back into the hole in the middle of his face.

'Klausy, you're reinstated,' Tension said sweetly. 'Can you forgive me? You've always been my number one really.'

'Just give me the audio files and I'll make up the Vox Spots,' Klaus instructed.

Kurt handed his brother a small Dictaphone, which Klaus connected to the USB port on his laptop computer. As Klaus played back the recorded voices, each one produced a distinctive saw-toothed trace on the screen. His single thick eyebrow sank down over his beady eyes as he tapped furiously at the keyboard.

Eventually a slot on the side of the laptop spat out two black discs, about the size of pennies.

'So how do those things work?' asked Kurt, his single eye narrowing with curiosity.

'Simple,' Klaus announced, with an air of superiority. 'Everyone's voice has a unique sound – like an audio fingerprint. Just one word is enough to define someone's precise vocal identity. The software I developed analyses the exact frequencies of each voice and imprints that information on to one of these.' Klaus held up one of the black discs on the end of his forefinger. 'Using tiny electrical impulses, the Vox Spot will modify the sound waves in the larynx to exactly mimic the sound of anyone's voice.'

'Amazing,' said Kurt.

'I simply refuse to take *all* the credit for the idea,' said Tension, taking the black disc from Klaus. 'I mean, without your brother doing the repetitive number-crunching, it may have taken me a few weeks longer to perfect the Vox Spots.'

Klaus looked incredulous. 'I wrote the whole program!'

Tension pressed the black spot on to her throat where it stuck. When she spoke again her voice had been transformed into that of a teenager. 'Of course you did, Klausy.' She smiled sweetly. 'I provided the inspiration and you mucked in with the perspiration. That's what makes us such a good team. Where would I be without you to do my donkey work?'

Klaus ground his teeth into a smile.

'It's so weird hearing the kid's voice come out of your mouth,' Kurt giggled.

'For real.' Tension approached Kurt with a bouncy stride. 'Er, it's like, totally, like, weirding me out, man, you get me?'

'That's funny!' Kurt snorted and the yellow bogey shot out of the hole in his face and attached itself to his chin.

Tension was swaggering around the room while the brothers laughed at her antics. 'I ain't got nuffin to do so I'm just gonna hang out, staring at my mobile phone, d'ya know what I mean?'

'You're just like a real teenager!' Kurt wiped a tear from his eye. 'Except you look so old.'

Kurt's last word reverberated like the off-key chime of an old clock. Tension's piercing green eyes narrowed. Kurt froze. The yellow worm on his chin quivered.

When Tension spoke, her words were a brittle

whisper. 'Nobody calls me *old*.'

Kurt's Adam's apple bobbed.

Suddenly Tension smiled brightly. 'That reminds me, I'd better put my face on,' she said breezily.

Taking the memory card from Kurt's camera, she slid it into the back of the Face-mapping-quick-drying-liquid-latex-mask-gun. Selecting the photo of the person she was to impersonate, she turned the gun on herself and pulled the trigger, closing her eyes as the fine spray coated her skin.

'There.' Tension smiled, pulling on a black wig. 'How do I look?'

'Like an annoying kid,' said Klaus.

'Excellent,' said Tension, slipping her mask-gun into a rucksack. 'So you both know the plan?'

Klaus nodded. Kurt produced another mask-gun from a hold-all and cocked its silver chamber.

'OK. Get your disguises on and get ringside. Let's do this and let's do it right. I'm going to have some fun with our friendly undercover kid. But I'm going to make it quick – I can't *bear* the feel of this nylon suit against my skin a moment longer than is absolutely necessary. Very soon the whole world will be sorry Adam Winchester ever crossed Evelyn Tension.' The assassin threw her head back and let out a triumphant cackle, which the Vox Spot on her throat converted into an altogether less threatening teenage giggle.

'Good luck, Evelyn,' Klaus muttered.

Tension's laughter died suddenly. 'Honey, luck has got *nothing* to do with it.'

Chapter 15

Archie wandered casually along the edge of the mats towards the two boxing rings and sat down on one of the benches, as he carefully scanned the crowd. A moment later a kid with spiky black hair appeared and sat next to him. Archie chin-jerked him before unwinding the bandages wrapped tightly around his hands. He had noticed many of the boys anxiously adjusting their bandages. It seemed to be a ritual display rather than a necessary function, but it created the impression of someone who was meticulously prepared for battle.

The sound of Highwater's clipped voice in his earpiece interrupted Archie's thoughts.

'All agents from IC. Skywalker is in the building.' The

133

mention of Toby Winchester's codename made the hairs on the back of Archie's neck stand up. Suddenly the mission felt very real. 'Skywalker is entering the arena through the southern ingress,' Highwater continued. 'Two PPOs are in attendance. All agents maintain vigilance and report any suspicious activity.'

Archie's eyes instinctively locked on the southern entrance where a lean figure, wearing a tracksuit and a black baseball cap, entered the arena. He was followed closely by two Personal Protection Officers, dressed casually in jumpers and jeans. As Toby Winchester anonymously walked passed the crowd Archie detected a slight ripple of activity from some individuals. A man in a navy anorak lowered his paper momentarily and a young woman waving a flag suddenly produced a camera phone. Were they members of the public who happened to have recognised the Prime Minister's son or undercover agents monitoring their comms channel? Or was one of them a highly trained assassin waiting for the perfect moment to strike?

Archie's body was tingling with anticipation and fear. Fear was OK, though. His father had always told him that nothing focuses the mind quite like a double dose of terror.

'That's Toby Winchester, that is,' the spiky-haired kid observed.

Archie wasn't sure if it was the mention of Winchester's name or the fact that someone had actually spoken to him that surprised him more.

'What? As in the Prime Minister's son?' he asked with a dubious sneer.

'That's the one.' The boy answered, untucking the end of one bandage and unwinding it rapidly.

'How d'you know that?' Archie said, turning to his neighbour.

The boy smiled wryly. 'Cos I'm fighting him in the first round, that's why. I've seen him at a few competitions. He's pretty good.'

'D'you think you can beat him?'

The boy's dark eyes twinkled. 'Course I can, man,' he bragged. 'I'm gonna take him down so hard he won't know what's hit him, you get me? Toby Winchester will be sorry we ever met. He's a dead man, man.'

Archie held the boy's gaze – looking deep into his dark pupils. He laughed nervously but the boy's expression remained completely serious.

'Mind you, if I knock out the Prime Minister's son I'll probably get bumped off by the SAS,

135

you know what I mean?'

Archie's throat suddenly constricted. Was the kid simply joking about the SAS – or did he know they were present? Archie felt the blood draining from his face as it occurred to him he might actually be talking to Evelyn Tension.

Archie peered closely at the boy's widow's peak and aquiline nose, wondering if they were real or just another elaborate latex disguise. The boy frowned and Archie realised he needed to get a grip, quickly.

'Definitely!' He smiled weakly and pointed to the roof, his finger trembling slightly. 'There's probably loads of snipers up there waiting to take you out if you don't let him win.'

'Tell me about it.' The boy's spiky head nodded and he mimed a sniper firing off a couple of rounds. Standing up he said, 'Listen I've got to go and warm up – my bout starts in half an hour.' The boy gave Archie the chin-jerk. 'Catch ya later.'

Archie jerked his chin back and watched the boy walk away, his shoulders rolling with each stride. 'Maybe I'll catch *you* later,' he muttered.

Leaning his elbows on his knees, Archie hung his head to speak discreetly into his comms kit. 'IC, this is Agent

Yankee,' he murmured. 'Skywalker's first opponent may be Tension. Suspect verbally threatened to take Skywalker down and seemed aware of potential SWAT-team presence. I recommend immediate interception and interrogation.'

'Copy that, Yankee,' Highwater replied.

For a moment Archie heard nothing. He imagined Highwater relaying his suspicions to her boss, who would probably dismiss them out of hand. Meanwhile the boy had nearly reached the changing rooms, where Toby Winchester was preparing for his first match.

Then Archie heard the voice of Hugh Figo on the common channel. 'Units Four and Seven, intercept Pravin Malik. I say again, intercept Pravin Malik.'

Through the corner of his eye Archie watched as four men immediately surrounded the boy. Two grabbed him roughly from behind, a third pressed something into his belly, while the fourth snapped a pair of handcuffs on his wrists. Then he was swiftly led out of sight.

'Suspect has been detained,' Figo announced.

'Nice work, Yankee,' said Gemma on the dedicated STINKBOMB channel. Archie glanced at her and she gave him a furtive thumbs-up signal.

'And the fox is in the bear trap,' Barney added.

'Zip it, Zulu,' snapped Highwater.

Archie exhaled a long breath. He wondered if the operation really was over. Something told him things had gone too smoothly. If Evelyn Tension really was such a master of disguise would she have threatened Toby Winchester as openly as Pravin Malik had? Unless her brazen behaviour had in fact been a double bluff . . . The idea that he had just been chatting with a highly dangerous killer made his arms and legs feel like jelly but he felt a sense of immense relief and pride that he may have just averted a deadly attack.

Suddenly a hand gripped him firmly by the shoulder. Archie spun round to see Ivan's flat face grinning at him.

'There you are, Hook,' Ivan leered. 'I've been looking for you everywhere.'

'Except here, obviously,' Archie offered lamely. 'What's up?'

'Well, you know I told you there was about as much chance of you winning the lottery as boxing today?'

Archie nodded guardedly.

'Well, I'd buy myself a ticket if I was you, son. Looks like it's your lucky day!'

Chapter 16

As Ivan escorted Archie to the changing rooms he explained that three boxers in his weight division had come down with food poisoning since having kippers for breakfast at a local hotel.

'Get warmed up,' Ivan instructed sternly. 'You're on in eight minutes.'

His mind spinning, Archie wandered into the boys' locker room. At the far end Toby Winchester was warming up, thumping combinations of punches into a pair of pads being held up by his trainer, who Archie assumed was also his personal bodyguard.

Archie pulled on his boxing gloves and tightened the Velcro wrist-straps with his teeth. Karate was his specialist combat sport but he had taken various other self-defence classes. He had sparred in a boxing ring a couple of times and he tried to remember what he'd been taught.

Keep your guard up and your chin down! he remembered his instructor barking at him. *You're not in the dojo now!*

In karate the fighters hold their hands at waist level and Archie reminded himself that a boxer's gloves should always protect his head. He threw a couple of left jabs followed by a straight right cross but everything felt awkward. The looser stance of karate felt so much more natural to him. He tried another couple of combinations.

'You're kidding me, right?' someone snorted.

Archie looked to the end of the room where Toby Winchester had taken a break from his warm-up to watch him. He was tall and lean, his blond hair was shaved down to a number three and one of his eyebrows was raised in an expression of utter disdain.

'I'm sorry?' Archie enquired. 'Were you talking to me?'

'I mean this has to be a joke, right?' Toby continued, his voice deep and sneering. 'This guy couldn't punch his way through a page of the *Daily Telegraph*.'

Archie realised Toby Winchester wasn't talking to

140

him after all – just about him.

'I mean,' Winchester continued, 'kids like him shouldn't be allowed to compete at my level. It just makes a mockery of the whole event.'

'I was only a reserve but some people dropped out,' Archie offered pleasantly. 'I didn't quite make the original cut.'

'Well that's no surprise!' Winchester brayed, looking at his trainer. 'They'd be better off scrapping the bout rather than fielding a no-hoper though. This guy's seriously going to get his block knocked off. I mean it's not fair on their opponents, if you ask me. Whoever fights this kid could end up doing him some serious harm – and I mean *see-ree-us*! Nobody wants to be responsible for some other loser's safety.'

Some of us don't have a choice, Archie thought.

Archie threw a few more combinations of punches, trying to ignore the puerile sniggers from the other side of the changing room. He was beginning to relax into the unfamiliar stance when one of the games officials came to tell him it was time to get into the ring. Removing his glasses and slipping them into his rucksack, Archie followed the official into the public arena.

'All units from Yankee,' he whispered – the tiny transceiver in his ear relaying his words to the other agents. 'Skywalker is in the changing rooms. Monitor entrance closely.'

'Skywalker's trainer is Special Forces,' Highwater replied. 'He's safe and sound.'

'Good for him,' Archie mumbled as he walked nervously past the martial-arts mats. He swallowed and climbed through the ropes and on to the springy canvas of the boxing ring.

Archie couldn't quite work out how he'd found himself in this situation. He was only meant to be a reserve, but now he was standing in the middle of a boxing ring facing Dougie McLeish, a snarling red-haired boy with baboon-like arms. If Malik was Evelyn Tension then there was no need for him to keep up this pretence. But Archie understood that until Malik had been confirmed as the assassin, Operation Gumshield was still very much active and he couldn't risk blowing his cover.

Archie jigged about a bit, removed his dressing gown, had a squirt of water and squared up to his growling pitbull of an opponent.

His head was buzzing so loudly he didn't hear a

word the referee said. Then the bell rang and Dougie held out a glove in a sporting gesture. Archie bumped the glove with his, then bounced back on the balls of his feet.

Springing from side to side Archie threw a couple of straight left jabs while his adversary advanced. Dougie blocked the first with his glove and ducked the second. Archie threw more punches and pranced around the ring, circling his opponent. Hunched low with his hands at head height Dougie stalked him relentlessly, watching his every move between his gloves.

Growing in confidence, Archie started to put together more combinations of punches but they were all blocked or didn't make contact at all. For over a minute and a half Archie danced and threw punches while Dougie paced after him, without firing any back.

'Does this guy know he's supposed to box you?' Barney's voice chirruped in Archie's earpiece. 'You must be way ahead on points.'

'This guy's not worried about the points, though,' Gemma stated. 'He's looking for a stoppage.'

'I just can't penetrate his guard,' Archie panted.

'Can't you use some of your karate?' Barney asked.

'I could flatten him with a roundhouse kick or a

143

'sweep,' Archie puffed, firing out a left-right combination that landed harmlessly on Dougie's forearms. 'But I don't think the Queensberry Rules allow for that.'

'What about working his body?' Gemma suggested. 'Get in close and use your uppercut.'

Archie was blowing hard now, his lungs heaving in his chest. For over two minutes he had skipped around the ring throwing punches constantly and his arms were starting to feel sluggish. Taking Gemma's advice he stepped forward, ducking to the right as he unleashed a savage uppercut to his opponent's stomach. Dougie dropped one arm across his body and swatted Archie's fist away with a look of disdain.

Archie pushed off his front foot to skip back to a safe distance but fatigue was setting in and he wasn't moving as nimbly as he had been. Dougie, who had conserved his energy up till now, reacted to Archie's sluggish retreat, suddenly exploding with venom and power. Launching himself forward, Dougie twisted his torso and whipped an arm over the top of Archie's gloves, dropping his right fist on to Archie's cheek like a bomb.

'Look out!' Gemma screamed but it was too late.

The punch felt like a cricket ball slamming into

Archie's face. The flesh of his cheek was pummelled against his teeth and a warm salty fluid leaked into his mouth. Staggering backwards, Archie tried to protect his face but his arms were flailing feebly and no match for Dougie's heavy artillery. The second punch came from the left, snapping Archie's chin to the side, where it was sent back again almost immediately by another thump from the right.

Archie was vaguely aware of the ropes pressing into his back but as the thunderous blows hammered into his head and stomach he felt strangely peaceful. His head dropped and all he could see was a blur of gloves and tangled arms and legs. Then he toppled over, crumpling into a heap as his head bounced off the canvas and the lights went out.

The next thing Archie knew, he was sitting on a stool in the corner of the ring. His gloves were off, his arms were spread and resting on the ropes and he was slumped back on the ringpost. His vision was blurry but he could just recognise Gemma kneeling in front of him with a first-aid kit open next to her. Numerous faces crowded out the ceiling as they peered down at him. The fight, the Student Games and Operation Gumshield came

145

flooding back. Leaning forward to rest his elbows on his knees, he tried to smile but his top lip felt fat and numb. 'What are you doing here, Vanessa Wallis?' he mumbled, his hair flopping into his eyes.

'I was worried about you, Danny Hook,' Gemma whispered.

'Thanks.' Archie nodded. 'Don't take this the wrong way but considering you are only a first-aider . . . is there any chance you could make room for, like, an actual doctor to take a look at me?'

'The match doctor is on his way,' Gemma replied.

Archie heard Barney's voice in his earpiece. 'How are you doing, Yankee?'

'Tired,' Archie whispered. 'I've been flat out.'

'At least you took it on the chin. Did you enjoy it?'

'Oh yeah. After two minutes in the ring I was hooked.'

Barney chuckled. 'You were a knockout.'

Just then the blur of concerned faces parted and the tall, fat match doctor knelt down and started prodding Archie with his cold sausagey fingers. After a few minutes of gentle requests and affirmative uh-huhs, while shining lights into every hole in Archie's head, Dr Thomas pronounced his verdict.

'Well, young man, I don't think you're concussed but it certainly looks like you've sustained a number of forceful blows to your head.'

'D'you think?' Archie asked sardonically.

The doctor prescribed aspirin and rest, and Archie felt a strong grip underneath one arm as he was levered to his feet. 'Come on, sunshine.'

Archie could just make out Ivan's featureless profile as he helped him back to the changing rooms and sat him on a bench.

'You just sit here and keep sipping,' said Ivan, handing Archie a bottle of water. 'The doctor will come back in about half an hour to check you over.'

As Ivan's fuzzy form receded towards the door Archie fumbled in his rucksack for his spectacles and slid them on. Toby Winchester was no longer warming up in the locker room and Archie assumed he must have gone into the arena to complete his preparations ringside. Archie's head was pounding as he leaned it gently against the wall behind him. I'm not sure I could possibly feel any worse right now, he thought.

Then a voice in his earpiece proved him wrong.

Chapter 17

'Attention, all units,' Hugh Figo ordered. 'Pravin Malik is clean. I say again, Malik is clean. Tension is still at large. Maintain positions and stay alert. Skywalker is due in the ring in ten.'

Archie felt strangely embarrassed that his suspicions about Malik had proved misguided. He'd thought he'd cracked the case but actually he'd simply diverted the Secret Service's attention away from the real villain – wherever she was hiding. A sense of abject despair sunk through him and he closed his eyes as if to shut himself away from his failings.

No more than a couple of minutes passed before he heard the changing-room door swing open and his head snapped upright instinctively. Although not

148

completely sharp, his vision was already much clearer and he smiled when he saw Gemma enter.

'Oh, there you are,' she said.

'Don't look so surprised,' Archie smiled. 'What's up?'

Gemma shrugged. 'Just doing a routine sweep. How are you feeling?'

'I'd feel a lot better if I hadn't screwed up.'

Gemma nodded. 'Don't feel bad. Your hunch was worth a shot. She's close – I can feel it. If we don't find her soon she'll slip away faster than you can say "Speedboat down the Thames".'

As Archie started to nod, a sharp pain shot down his neck and he grimaced.

'You need to close your eyes for a while,' Gemma suggested. 'I'll call you if anything comes up.'

Archie leaned his head back and allowed his eyelids to shut. He heard the changing-room door swing open, then close. Then it was quiet.

He had no idea how long he'd been asleep when he was disturbed by someone bursting into the locker room. He opened his eyes to see Pravin Malik stride past him.

'All right?' Archie slurred.

'Not really, man.' Malik laughed. 'But on balance I'm better than you though. What happened? You look like you were hit by a truck.'

Archie nodded. 'A truck called Dougie McLeish.'

'Ah well, no shame there. He's brutal, man.'

'You don't say.' Archie smiled. 'Anyway aren't you supposed to be boxing?'

'They agreed a ten-minute delay – sort of.' Malik sounded agitated. 'My whole routine's out of whack though. I got arrested by some guys from MI5 or 6 or whatever. They cuffed me and asked me all these questions, took my prints and samples of skin and everything.'

'No way!' Archie immediately thought he'd overdone his surprise but Malik was too het up to notice.

'Anyway they let me go but I've got no time to warm up. I've just got to grab my gloves from my locker and go.'

'Well, good luck.' Archie held up a fist. 'Let him have it.'

Closing his eyes and leaning his head back again, Archie listened to Pravin Malik's footsteps recede to the rear of the changing room. The sole of his boxing shoes squeaked on the shiny floor as he turned the corner at the end of the passage and took four more steps before stopping. Archie heard the clunk of the key turning the deadlock, and then the rattling sound of Malik struggling to open his locker. Finally came the metallic twang of the door popping open.

'Hey!' Malik yelped.

A dull clanging noise echoed round the changing room for a few seconds, as if someone was beating sheet metal with their hand. Then silence.

Archie sat upright, eyes darting about as he strained his ears for any clues about what was happening.

'Are you OK?' he enquired.

There was no answer.

'Pravin?' he called, a slight tremor in his voice. 'Are you all right?'

Again there was no reply.

Archie jumped to his feet, trying to ignore the pounding in his head, and crept along the corridor of lockers towards the back of the room. As he neared the T-junction at the end he could hear an indistinct sound from round the corner, like someone shuffling about.

It's almost like a body being dragged along the floor, he thought chillingly.

Whatever grisly fate had befallen Pravin Malik

outside his locker, Archie would have to face it. Feeling a giddying mix of total terror and a powerful sense of duty, he raised his hands in preparation for battle.

OK, he thought resolutely. Whoever you are, you've picked the wrong guy to mess with today.

With that emotion swelling his chest Archie leaped from his hiding place, adopting the wide-legged crouch and open-palmed stance of a deadly ninja. Then he froze as he came face to face with the person lurking outside Malik's locker.

Pravin Malik was dressed for the ring in his white silk dressing gown and blue boxing gloves. Slightly stooped, with his hands raised, he was warming up for his match by throwing some gentle punches at an imaginary opponent. He was wearing a pair of white headphones, which explained why he hadn't responded to Archie's calls.

As he skipped forward his back foot scuffed the floor, making the shuffling sound Archie had identified as a body being dragged along. Seeing Archie poised for action, Malik dropped his hands and smiled.

'Who do you think you are?' he said, taking his headphones out of his ears. 'Jackie Chan?'

Blushing, Archie relaxed his stance. 'I heard you

shout "Hey"' He shrugged. 'I thought maybe you were in trouble.'

Malik laughed. 'Oh yeah. I thought someone had nicked my gloves but they were under a load of other stuff. I get worked-up, man, what can I say?'

'Oh yeah, I totally get that,' Archie insisted. 'I'm totally wired before I box. Like, totally.' He smiled weakly, hoping he'd sounded convincing.

'OK.' Malik smiled uncertainly. 'Listen, I've got to get out there and fight but you take it easy, man.'

Archie nodded and held out a fist.

Malik reached out an arm, gently bumping his glove against Archie's knuckles. As he did so, something caught Archie's eye. It was only for a fraction of a second but it was enough to freeze the blood in his veins.

'You OK, man?' Malik asked. 'You look like you've seen a ghost.'

Quickly Archie shook his head and smiled. 'Just feeling a bit dizzy, that's all.'

'You need to kick back, man,' Malik suggested, heading towards the door. 'I'll be back in five – after I've murdered Toby Winchester.'

As Archie watched the boy's shoulders rolling away from him he felt a torrent of panic rising inside him.

Had he really seen what he thought he'd seen? Or had his blurry vision been playing tricks on him? Closing his eyes he pictured Pravin Malik's fist bumping his and what he saw left him in no doubt.

As Malik's arm had extended towards him, about four inches of the skin on his forearm had been exposed – between his glove and the sleeve of his dressing gown. His skin had been smooth where it protruded from the cuff, but where it met the glove it had been wrinkled, as though it had ridden up somehow. Like a tight-fitting sleeve that had been pushed back, the skin hadn't covered all of Malik's wrist. And Archie was sure that the inch in between had been made of metal, entwined with wires and circuitry. It seemed almost too bizarre to comprehend but there was only one conclusion to be drawn: Pravin Malik had a mechanical arm.

As Archie hurried towards the arena, Malik's final words echoed hauntingly in his head.

I'll be back in five – after I've murdered Toby Winchester.

Chapter 18

An incredible roar erupted from the crowd as Archie entered the arena through the south entrance.

'What's the fuss about?' he demanded, touching his earpiece.

'Darth Vader is in the building,' Gemma replied.

'What? Right now?' Archie's voice was taut with anxiety. The Prime Minister had arrived and Pravin Malik was on the loose. And this time Archie was sure Malik was an impostor.

'That's affirmative,' Barney chipped in. 'The kingfisher has dropped in to watch his lion cub, er . . . boxing.'

'What's his location?' Archie asked, scanning the banked seating.

'North-east entrance,' Gemma replied. 'He's with four PPOs and there's about fifty undercover operatives in his seating block.'

Beyond the martial-arts areas and between the boxing rings Archie saw a slim figure in a navy suit and green tie acknowledging the crowd with a regal wave as he took his seat in the front row. Shortening his focus, Archie saw Malik's rolling gait approaching the boxing ring, where Toby Winchester was already running through his final pre-match warm-up.

Archie strode out briskly and touched his earpiece. 'All units, this is Agent Yankee,' he announced. 'This is a Priority One. I have a positive ID on the suspect who is approaching Vader and Skywalker and must be intercepted without delay.'

'Yankee, this is Figo.' Archie felt relieved that Hugh Figo was listening. On his command Pravin Malik would be crushed by a mountain of Special Forces soldiers. 'Can you identify the suspect and describe the nature of the threat?'

'The suspect is . . .' Archie paused, realising his credibility was about to crumble beneath him. 'The suspect is Pravin Malik?' he said, unable to keep the question mark out of his voice.

156

'Is this some sort of joke, Yankee?' Figo's voice blared. 'Malik has already been detained and questioned. He is clean.'

Archie stepped up his pace as Malik neared the boxing ring. 'But that's not the real Malik. It's an impostor. He has a mechanical arm, sir,' he protested, recoiling inwardly at how ridiculous his claim sounded.

'I can assure you, Yankee, that Malik was given a thorough physical examination and was found to be in possession of precisely no mechanical arms.'

'But—'

'No buts, agent Yankee,' Figo roared. 'If you have some personal vendetta against Pravin Malik, then I suggest you slug it out with him like a man.'

As Pravin Malik came within yards of the boxing ring Archie broke into a jog. 'Sir, this is a matter of life and death. You have to stop—'

'How dare you tell me how to run my operation, you impertinent *child*,' Figo's voice quavered with simmering rage. 'I have over a hundred *real* agents positioned around the venue who are all highly trained field personnel but you expect me to focus my attention on your schoolboy fantasy about some bionic man?'

'It's not a fantasy, sir—'

'That was a rhetorical question!' Figo exploded. 'You are obviously still dazed from the thrashing you took in the ring and incapable of rational thought. You are hereby removed from this operation . . . and suspended from duty immediately.'

'But—'

'Stand down, Agent Yankee! That is an order.'

Hugh Figo's reaction took the wind out of Archie's sails and he stopped for a moment, feeling strangely alone amidst thousands of cheering people. He glanced across to see Gemma kneeling ringside and looking sadly over at him. In the press enclosure Barney lowered his camera and shook his head sympathetically.

That's it, Archie thought. There's nothing more I can do.

But as he watched Pravin Malik being reminded about his timekeeping by the ringside judge Archie felt a spark of resolve in his belly. He had to trust his instincts.

Like a sprinter bursting out of his blocks Archie broke into a run, pumping his fists furiously as he pelted across the crash mats. He weaved between two judges and hurdled a pile of sports bags. Pravin Malik was just fifteen metres away and Archie had a clear path ahead of him. Nothing could stop him now, he thought, as Malik turned to climb into the ring.

'Tango Six has contact with a young male approaching Darth Vader and Skywalker.'

In his adrenalin-charged euphoria Archie thought the transmission from an anonymous undercover agent referred to Malik.

'Take him down.'

'Copy that.'

Yes! Archie thought, as he hurtled towards the ring. Take him down now!

Archie didn't see the burly SAS sergeant swing his arm horizontally into his chest but it felt as if he'd run into the bough of an oak tree. The force of the blow lifted him off his feet, which flailed into the air, as his head and shoulders crashed backwards on to the ground. A knee drove into his solar plexus, expelling all the breath from his lungs and a hand grabbed his throat tightly, preventing any more air coming in.

As Archie's eyes bulged open he recognised the flattened face snarling down at him.

'Ivan,' he croaked. 'You've got to let me go. I'm with MI6.'

'No I don't,' Ivan growled. 'And so am I.'

'That's not the real Pravin Malik,' Archie choked. 'He's got a mechanical arm.'

'Yeah. And I'm Steve Austin.'

Archie looked up at Ivan's smug grin and frowned. 'Who's Steve Austin?' He felt Ivan squeezing his throat more tightly and the edges of his vision began to darken and close in. Over Ivan's shoulder he saw Pravin Malik climbing into the ring with Toby Winchester. Through a black tunnel Archie watched Malik duck under the rope, then turn and catch his eye. As the tunnel closed in Archie was sure he saw Malik wink, then for the second time that day, the lights went out.

Chapter 19

Archie opened his eyes and squinted into a bright white light. Turning his head reflexively he saw Gemma sitting beside him. He was flat on his back on a bed, enclosed by a plastic curtain.

'Where am I?' he whispered.

'Er, the medical bay?' Gemma said as though it was the most obvious thing in the world.

'How long was I out?'

Gemma pursed her lips solemnly. 'Two days.'

Archie sat upright and swung his legs over the edge of the bed. 'Two days!?' he yelped – then he noticed Gemma's deadpan expression. 'You're winding me up, aren't you?'

Gemma nodded. 'About five minutes actually. That

SAS guy put you out with a chokehold and St John's brought you here. Highwater told me to stay with you and make sure you don't get into any more trouble.'

Archie reached forward and swished the curtain open. 'Where's the doctor?' he asked, scanning the clinically sparse room.

'He's ringside,' Gemma said. 'In case you'd forgotten, the PM's son is boxing Pravin Malik as we speak.'

'Malik!' Archie exclaimed, sliding off the couch on to his feet. 'We have to stop the fight.'

Gemma placed a palm firmly on Archie's chest. 'I think you've done enough for one day. Our orders are to sit tight and that's what we're going to do.'

'But Malik is an impostor,' Archie insisted. 'He's got a metal arm, Gemma. I saw it myself. I think he's one of Tension's henchmen or something.'

Gemma listened carefully to Archie's theory, then touched her earpiece. 'X-ray to Zulu,' she said. 'How's the fight going?'

Barney's reply was immediate and solemn. 'Zulu to X-ray – the panther is hungry but the platypus is elusive, over.'

'OK, Master Shifu.' Gemma rolled her eyes at Archie. 'Is there any chance you can speak in, like, a normal

162

sentence? How is Skywalker doing?'

'Skywalker's doing pretty good,' Barney replied. 'He landed one punch on Malik's chin that looked like a certain KO. How he didn't go down I'll never know. They're just about to start the last round. I'd say it's all square so far.'

Gemma looked at Archie with an expression that said 'I told you so'.

'I know what I saw, Gem,' Archie said sulkily, 'The guy had some sort of circuitry in his arm.'

'Maybe it was just a tattoo or something,' Gemma suggested. 'But if an assassin was posing as Pravin Malik so that he could kill Toby Winchester, do you think he'd wait until the third round of their match before smoking him?'

Archie shrugged reluctantly. 'Dunno. Suppose not.'

Gemma placed her hand on Archie's arm. 'Everybody makes mistakes,' she whispered. 'It's cool that you were committed enough to follow through on your suspicions.'

Archie pulled a face. 'I'm not sure Huge Ego will see it that way.'

'Don't worry about him,' Gemma said reassuringly. 'Highwater will look after you. She may be strict but she's pretty fair too. There's no way she'll hang you out to dry for this.'

Archie thought Gemma was probably right. He wouldn't get kicked out of STINKBOMB for this, but he still felt sick. How could he have made such a big mistake? Concluding he must have been concussed after all, and imagined the robotic arm, Archie slumped back on the bed, feeling like a total loser.

Just as his head touched the pillow an almighty roar erupted in the stadium outside the door. It was a cry of shock and horror, multiplied by thousands and magnified by the acoustics of the domed roof. Archie snapped upright, the floor almost vibrating beneath his trainers as he leaped to his feet.

Barney's voice was shrieking in his ear. 'HOLY COW! UN-BELIEVABLE!'

'Zulu, this is Yankee,' Archie said urgently. 'What's happening out there?'

'I've never seen a punch like it!' Barney exclaimed.

'Zulu, this is X-ray.' Gemma stated sternly. '*What* happened?'

'He actually lifted him off the floor with a single punch! I'm surprised his head didn't come clean off. He flew across the ring like a rag doll.'

'Zulu,' said Archie firmly. 'Who punched who?'

'Skywalker,' Barney gabbled. 'Malik.'

'Can you confirm that Skywalker punched Malik?' Gemma said slowly.

Archie held his breath as they waited for Barney's reply.

'Negative,' he said. 'Malik punched Skywalker. Skywalker is down. I repeat, Skywalker is down.'

Archie immediately made a move for the door. Stepping across his path, Gemma crossed her arms and cocked her head. 'Where do you think you're going?'

'We've got to go and help,' Archie pleaded.

Gemma shook her head emphatically. 'There's nothing we can do to help Toby Winchester now. We're just going to follow our orders and wait here.'

'But—' Archie protested, but Gemma cut him short with a death stare.

The two of them stood in silence listening to Barney's frantic ringside commentary, which came in sporadic bursts like radio newsflashes.

'Everyone's trying to crowd into the ring . . . The Secret Service dudes are keeping them back . . . Darth Vader is reaching through the ropes – calling Skywalker's name . . . The medics are all over him . . . They're putting

165

him on oxygen . . . The doctor's checking his pulse . . . They've got him on a stretcher . . . He's on his way to the medical bay.'

Archie and Gemma stared at each other in shock, both unable to speak. Seconds later the door burst open and the commotion from outside poured into the room.

Two burly ambulance men – one bald, one with curly black hair – jogged in carrying Toby Winchester on a stretcher – an oxygen mask strapped over his nose and mouth. Hurrying alongside them was Dr Thomas, his tummy bouncing over his belt as he puffed for air. Immediately behind the stretcher was the Prime Minister himself, Adam Winchester, whose face was slack with worry. The PM was flanked by four plain-clothes officers all talking into hidden microphones.

The doctor ushered the stretcher into a separate room at the back of the medical bay, then turned to address Adam Winchester as he attempted to enter the room.

'I'm sorry, Prime Minister,' the doctor said kindly. 'I need a few moments to examine your son alone. I'll let you know when you can come in.'

Adam Winchester nodded and stepped backwards out of the room, followed by the bald ambulance man.

Dr Thomas closed the door.

Folding his arms tightly across his chest, the Prime Minister started pacing the room, walking to within a metre of Archie and Gemma before stopping. He paused for a moment, catching Archie's eye briefly, then he turned and paced back the other way.

In that short moment of eye contact the Prime Minister had reminded Archie of his dad. Instead of the self-assured leader of the country, Archie had seen a vulnerable human being – a loving father worried sick about his son. But, more than that, there had been something else about him that felt familiar to Archie. Finally, Dr Thomas emerged from the private room and everyone turned to him.

'Prime Minister, your son is going to be fine,' he said softly. 'You may see him now but he is sleeping. He'll have a headache for a few days but he'll make a full recovery.'

'Oh, that's marvellous news.' Smiling broadly, the Prime Minister unfolded his arms and entered the private room. As the door closed behind him, one of the undercover officers positioned himself in front of it like a sentry. After a couple of minutes Adam Winchester walked back out, beaming and thanking

167

Dr Thomas for his excellent care.

As he strode towards the exit Adam Winchester stopped in front of Archie and Gemma. Grinning happily he reached out and shook their hands in turn.

'St John's does some excellent work,' he said to Gemma, while he urged Archie to 'Get well soon'.

Then, surrounded by his personal bodyguards, he went back out to the sports arena where scores of press photographers' flashbulbs greeted his emergence.

Among the crowd of reporters waiting for Adam Winchester was Barney, busy snapping away.

'I am happy to report that my son is going to be just fine,' Adam Winchester announced with a wide smile. 'He is concussed but he is in very good hands and I would like to thank all the medical staff at this event for the care they have shown him. Now if you'll excuse me –' the Prime Minister flamboyantly checked his watch – 'I have a very busy schedule today.'

Inside the medical bay, Archie and Gemma were listening to Adam Winchester's statement.

'He seems pretty cool,' Gemma mumbled. 'For a grown-up.'

'Suppose,' Archie replied, although something in the back of his mind was troubling him.

Chapter 20

In Conference Room 10, at the eastern perimeter of the O2 Arena, Helen Highwater was conducting STINKBOMB's mission debrief. Although the tournament was still going on and the spectators' distant cheers were drifting occasionally into earshot, MI6's interest in the event was over. The Prime Minister had been safely escorted to his helicopter, which had taken him to his next ministerial appointment. Toby Winchester had been taken by air ambulance to the Royal Chelsea and Westminster hospital where he was recovering in a private ward with an armed police guard.

The only event that was even slightly out of the ordinary was that Pravin Malik had not been seen since his bout with Toby – but his disappearance wasn't being treated as suspicious. He was simply presumed to have mingled with the crowd and slipped away, in case he got into trouble for flattening the PM's kid.

Archie, Barney and Gemma were sitting in a row while Highwater stood in front of them, shadowed by Holden Grey.

'So, all in all, I think we can declare our mission accomplished,' Highwater announced, 'although certain individuals' actions were, shall we say, somewhat cavalier.' She glared over her spectacles at Archie, who pursed his lips and nodded.

'What were you thinking, charging at Pravin Malik like that?' Highwater reprimanded. 'It's lucky Sergeant Small intercepted you or we'd have had a lot of explaining to do, young man.'

'FIY, Agent Yankee,' Holden Grey chipped in. 'You have to be as cool as a courgette in the field or your cover will be blown faster than you can say Dozy Rascal. Do you get me?'

Archie looked blankly at his superiors but his thoughts were elsewhere.

'Agents X-ray and Zulu,' Highwater continued. 'You both carried out your duties to the letter and are to be commended. Agent Yankee, you have left me with the unenviable task of explaining to Hugh Figo . . . why you disobeyed a direct order from your superior.'

Archie shrugged wearily.

'How can you function as a member of STINKBOMB when you behave so erratically?' Highwater folded her arms. 'While your fellow agents are strictly following orders you are charging around like an overexcited bloodhound at the slightest whiff of suspicion.'

'Yes!' Archie exclaimed, clapping his hands.

'Well I'm glad you agree with me,' Highwater mumbled.

'No – I wasn't agreeing with you.' Archie sprang out of his chair.

'Excuse me?' Highwater said tersely.

'I've just realised something,' Archie explained, holding his palms upward. 'It's been bugging me for ages, then the penny dropped when you mentioned the *whiff* of suspicion.'

'Spare us any more of your wild accusations, Yankee,' Highwater sighed.

'Please just give me thirty seconds to explain,' Archie pleaded.

Highwater relented, looking at her watch. 'Thirty seconds.'

'When Adam Winchester entered the medical bay, he came over to me and I caught his eye,' Archie explained excitedly. 'I felt weirdly close to him. Then I realised he really reminded me of my dad.'

'How touching,' said Highwater. 'Twenty seconds.'

'I couldn't work out what it was about him that was so familiar,' Archie continued. 'But I've just twigged why. He smelt just like my dad.'

'Well, they're both busy men,' said Highwater dismissively. 'It's no surprise if they both suffer from a little *body odour* on occasion. Ten seconds left.'

'Not that sort of smell,' Archie sighed. 'They use the same aftershave. It's called Distinction.'

'So they have the same taste in cologne.' Highwater smirked. 'I'd characterise that more as a coincidence than a threat to national security.'

'But *after* he'd been in to see his son he smelt different,' Archie said forcefully. 'He was wearing some kind of aftershave . . . but it definitely wasn't Distinction.'

Highwater had stopped counting and her mouth remained slightly open.

'I know politicians are vain,' Barney piped up. 'But what kind of person bothers to spray on new aftershave when he's visiting his son in the emergency room!'

172

'That's not what happened,' Gemma said flatly.

'Er, the dude came out smelling totally different. Where have you been for the last few minutes?' Barney shook his head disparagingly. 'Do pay attention, Agent X-ray.'

'Gemma means there's another explanation,' Archie reasoned. 'Remember Mr Grey saying that when someone tries to hide their identity, there's always something that gives them away? Well in this case it was the Distinction.'

'I see.' Barney nodded sagely. 'Meaning what?'

'Meaning that the Prime Minister that came out of that examination room was not the same one that went in.'

'If you're right, Yankee, this is serious,' Highwater announced gravely. 'But we need more evidence before we can act.'

'I'll go and check Malik's locker,' Archie announced. 'If I'm right I think I might find the real Pravin inside.'

'I'll go and scope out the examination room,' said Gemma.

'Good,' said Highwater. 'And Zulu, I want to see every single photo you have of the Prime Minister.'

As Archie turned to leave, Barney grabbed his arm

and whispered, 'This is so weird.'

Archie nodded. 'I know. It's almost unbelievable.'

'How long have we had two Prime Ministers?'

Archie studied his friend's blank expression for a moment. 'We don't have two Prime Ministers,' he said slowly. 'The one who came out of the medical room and is now running the country is an impostor – a double. I think we misunderstood Evelyn Tension's plan from the start.'

'Go on,' Highwater encouraged.

'We assumed Tension was planning to kill the Prime Minister's son to punish him for making her give up her family to become a Scalpel.' Archie scanned the expectant expressions in the room. 'But I think Adam Winchester was her target from the start. She just used Toby to get the PM on his own so she could make her switch. I have a horrible feeling she's actually planning something bigger – more devilish than assassinating his son.'

'Such as?' Gemma enquired.

Archie puffed out his cheeks and pushed his glasses up his nose. 'Who knows? If she, or one of her cronies, is pretending to be the PM then there's no limit to the mayhem they could cause.'

174

'Give us a worst-case scenario,' said Barney.

'Never mind worst-case, I'll give you a realistic scenario,' Highwater interrupted. 'If you're right, then Evelyn Tension has untold military power at her fingertips. A single command from her and we're talking about the end of the world.'

Chapter 21

When STINKBOMB regrouped, the conference room was filled with an air of urgency.

As expected, Archie had found Pravin Malik inside his locker. He was groggy and confused, and apparently had no recollection of anything that had happened that day. Archie had left Malik in the changing room accompanied by two paramedics and an MI6 agent who was waiting for the all-clear to question the kid.

Gemma's trip to the medical bay had proved equally interesting. Dr Thomas was nowhere to be seen. What she had found, however, rolled up and stuffed into the bottom of a medicine cabinet, was one St John's Ambulance uniform – men's large. Hidden inside it were a curly black wig and a fat-suit.

'Ten quid says our friendly Doctor Thomas was wearing this under his coat,' Gemma announced, dropping the padded leotard on to a desk.

'Another tenner says he wasn't a real doctor,' Archie agreed. 'And that wig looks suspiciously like one of the St John's Ambulance guys' hairdo.'

'Hair-don't, more like,' Gemma sneered.

Barney had plugged his digital SLR into a laptop and was studying the screen as his photos appeared.

'Radical,' Holden Grey said, squinting at the screen. 'How soon can you display them chronologically in the order they were taken?'

'Done,' Barney replied clicking the mouse. 'They're split into two events. Before the PM went into the medical bay on the left, and after he came out on the right.'

'OK, team' Highwater announced. 'Who fancies a game of Spot the Difference?'

Everyone gathered around the laptop, frowning in concentration at the photographs, but no matter how hard they tried no one could see anything obviously different.

'This is impossible,' Barney complained. 'The dudes are identical.'

177

'There must be something,' Grey encouraged. 'There's always something.'

'Wait!' Gemma yelped. Pushing between Archie and Barney she clicked away at the mouse, enlarging two pictures so that they filled the screen.

'Look!' she said, zooming in on the Prime Minister's wrist in each shot. 'Check out his watch. What's different?'

'Bingo,' Barney said immediately. 'His watch says it's twelve o'clock in this picture but *ten past* twelve in this one.'

'I'm pretty sure that's because you took the pictures ten minutes apart,' Archie suggested gently.

'How about his watch being on his left wrist in this one –' Gemma tapped the screen with her fingernail – 'but on the right in this one?'

'Oh yeah,' Barney blustered. 'I thought you meant what's different about it *apart* from obviously being on different wrists.'

'There isn't any doubt now.' Archie clenched his fists. 'There's no way the PM would have washed off his old aftershave, sprayed on a new one and swapped his watch over while visiting Toby in the medical bay. The guy the Secret Service ushered out of here was definitely an impostor.'

Holden Grey massaged his forehead. 'We'd better call Mr Figo and give him a heads-up with the low-down.'

'I agree,' said Highwater. 'But first we need to be clear about the sequence of events and have watertight evidence. Figo will tear open any holes in our theory.'

'First of all, the Pravin Malik who KO'd Toby Winchester was a fake,' Archie stated. 'The real Malik was replaced by someone with some sort of mechanical arm after the police had questioned him – possibly Tension herself. I think the impersonator was waiting inside Malik's locker and jumped him when he went to get his gloves. The real Malik was bundled into his locker so that the impostor could knock out the Prime Minister's son with her bionic fist.'

'I reckon Doctor Thomas has been fake all along,' offered Gemma.

Archie nodded. 'When Toby was floored, two St John's guys carried him into the examination room but only the bald one came out. The curly-haired one stayed in the room and must have been in on it too. When the Prime Minister went in to see his son, the phoney doctor and the ambulance man must have overpowered him with a sedative and then hidden him in the room.'

179

'What about Toby Winchester?' Gemma asked. 'Is there a chance he was switched as well?'

'Good question, X-ray,' Grey replied. 'I'll call the hospital and get them to run a DNA analysis on Toby's blood.'

'So,' Highwater announced firmly. 'It certainly appears that the paramedic swapped clothes with the PM and came out wearing a highly sophisticated Adam Winchester mask. If we're right and he is currently masquerading as the Prime Minister, then Evelyn Tension is effectively controlling the whole country.'

'Figo's going to ask what happened to the real PM,' Barney added, making out like he already knew the answer.

'This,' said Gemma emphatically, turning her laptop so the others could see the screen. 'It's CCTV footage from the corridor outside the medical bay, taken about half an hour after the fake Adam Winchester left the Dome and Toby had been taken to hospital.'

The grainy picture showed two figures wearing the fluorescent jackets of games officials leaving the medical bay. Walking closely side by side, the pair left the arena via the southern entrance, their heads covered by woollen hats.

'Where did they get the clothes from?' asked Archie.

'Doctor Thomas could have had all sorts of disguises hidden inside his fat suit,' Grey suggested. 'I'd wager he was also packing a piece which he jammed into the PM's ribs when he freely marched him out of here unhindered.'

'X-ray,' barked Highwater. 'I want you to track those two figures on the surveillance cameras. I want to know where they went when they left this building.'

'I'm on it,' Gemma replied, her fingers purring over her keyboard.

'There's one thing I don't understand,' Archie muttered. 'How did they change their disguises so quickly? The door to the examination room was only closed for about three minutes but we're saying that was enough time for that paramedic to remove his clothes and wig, dress up as the PM and put on a mask that was so realistic the world's press and the entire Secret Service didn't spot he's a fake. It's impossible.'

'Not with a Face-mapping-quick-drying-liquid-latex-mask-gun,' Highwater said grimly.

'You took the words right out of my mouth,' said Barney, nodding knowingly. 'It's the only explanation, in my book.'

181

'Which book is that?' Gemma muttered, keeping her eyes trained on her laptop screen. '*The Bumper Book of Spy Dot-to-Dot?*'

'What is a face-drying-mask-mapping-thingamy anyway?' Archie asked.

'Face-mapping-quick-drying-liquid-latex-mask-gun,' Holden Grey corrected. 'The idea has been floating about Tech Branch for decades but no one had ever perfected the technology to make it work. It's a hand-held device not dissimilar to the portable scanners they use in supermarkets.'

'That's right,' Highwater continued, 'but instead of scanning a barcode you use it to scan a human face – memorising every contour and every blemish. Then you point the device at someone else and spray their face with a thin film of quick-drying latex that exactly replicates the first person's features.'

'Narmsayin?' Grey cut in. 'MI6 built a prototype about ten years ago but it never quite hit the spot. Project Gemini was finally shelved about six years ago which, come to think of it, was about the time Agent Tension went AWOL without leave.'

'So you think Evelyn Tension has perfected the mask-gun?' Archie asked.

'It's distinctly possible,' Highwater surmised, tapping a pen against her teeth. 'If she managed to hack into the Tech Branch project files she could have stolen the blueprint for the mask-gun and someone with her IQ could have ironed out the flaws in the design. It would also explain why she's been able to so effectively elude MI6 for so long.'

'If she has,' said Archie, 'is it plausible that she could use it to masquerade as the Prime Minister?'

'Absolutely.' Highwater nodded grimly. 'She could masquerade as anyone she chooses. Mapping someone's face is as simple as taking a photograph and the mask takes seconds to apply. X-ray, any luck tracking down the suspects from the medical bay?'

Gemma's mouth pulled to one side and she shook her head. 'I lost them in the crowd – there's thousands of people out there. They could be anywhere by now.'

'Keep looking!' Highwater snapped. 'They must not be allowed to escape!'

Chapter 22

Everyone gathered behind Gemma, studying the surveillance footage from security cameras at the O2.

'How many cameras are there?' Barney asked.

'Hundreds,' Gemma answered gruffly. 'Literally hundreds.'

'If I was her I'd head for the tube,' Barney offered. 'Or the airport. Then again, maybe she'll trick us by staying on foot.'

Gemma rolled her eyes. 'Well, thanks for narrowing it down, Zulu.'

'She must be long gone by now,' Archie sighed. 'Once she had the PM she'd have scarpered faster than you can say "Speedboat down the Thames".'

'What's that supposed to mean?' Gemma muttered.

Archie felt suddenly awkward. 'I'm not really sure,' he admitted. 'It just sounded cool when you said it earlier.'

'Who? Me?'

'Yeah. When you came into the changing rooms, remember? I was recovering from my bout and you said if we didn't stop Tension soon she'd escape faster than I could say "Speedboat down the Thames".'

'You were hallucinating, clearly,' Gemma mumbled, leaning closer to the screen to study a particular person. 'I never saw you in the changing rooms.'

'Yes you did,' Archie laughed. 'You were doing a routine sw—' Archie didn't finish his sentence. He felt like someone had pressed a cold blade against his spine. The hairs all over his body were standing upright.

Gemma stopped typing and turned to look at him. Barney, Highwater and Grey waited in silence.

'If it wasn't you,' Archie concluded in a whisper. 'It must have been Evelyn Tension.'

'Or, indeed, one of her accomplices,' Highwater added.

'But how did she map Gemma's face?' Archie asked.

'The journalist who collared us when we arrived.' Barney clapped his hands loudly. 'He wasn't taking our pictures at all – he was mapping our faces.'

'And our voices, probably,' Gemma suggested.

''Tension probably went straight to Malik's locker to hide,' said Archie, excitedly adjusting his glasses. 'I closed my eyes and heard the door shut but I didn't actually *see* her leave. But she could have sneaked into the locker without me seeing her. Why bother even talking to me?'

'Because odious masterminds like Evelyn Tension can't resist showing off how clever they are,' Barney marvelled. 'Her scheme was probably going so smoothly she wanted to inject a bit of danger.'

'By talking to a concussed twelve-year-old?' Gemma scoffed. 'No offence, Archie, but you weren't exactly much of a threat at the time.'

'That wasn't the risk she was taking,' Archie exclaimed. 'The dangerous part was telling us how she planned to escape.'

'Speedboat down the Thames,' Barney muttered, his eyes shining. 'Classic!'

'X-ray, pull up footage from any jetty or marina nearby,' Highwater instructed.

Less than five minutes later Gemma whooped with delight.

'Bingo,' she said, tapping her laptop's screen. Everyone intently watched the video footage on the computer. 'This is from a security camera at a jetty about a mile downstream from the O2.'

On the screen two figures in bright yellow coats hurried down a gangplank on to a large motor launch that was moored by the boardwalk.

'Those are the guys who left the medical bay,' Gemma narrated. The two people climbed aboard the boat and went into the cabin. Gemma clicked her laptop's mouse and the footage began to fast-forward. 'The first two got to the boat about two hours ago,' she explained, clicking the video back to normal speed. 'This was taken about ten minutes later.'

A slender figure, wearing a bomber jacket and beanie hat, arrived at the boat and untied its mooring rope before climbing aboard.

'Check out the footwear,' whispered Gemma.

'Boxing shoes,' Archie commented.

'Exactly. Either this kid has come straight from 1986 or he's just been boxing in this competition.'

'Malik's impostor.' Highwater clenched a fist as she spoke. 'As we suspected.'

'Watch,' Gemma urged.

Reaching the doorway to the cabin, the kid pulled off his woollen hat and tossed his head back. Gemma tapped the mouse and the picture froze, as did everyone in the room.

Fascinated, Archie stared at the image on the screen. It showed the figure half inside the cabin, beanie hat in hand. The person's face was already hidden but flying back out of the door like a flame was a long mane of fiery red hair.

'Evelyn Tension,' he breathed. Archie thought about the conversations he'd had with Tension in the changing room – first posing as Gemma then as Malik, when he'd glimpsed the circuitry on his wrist. The idea that he'd been face-to-face alone with such a ruthless assassin made him shudder.

'She must have just blended into the crowd after she flattened Toby Winchester,' Gemma added. 'But if she's on the boat with the real PM, who's posing as Adam Winchester?'

'One of her stooges,' Barney said categorically. 'All *seriously* odious masterminds have a number of willing henchmen at their disposal. They are usually brutally strong but lacking the villain's mental power and willing to sacrifice themselves in order to fulfil their master's plan.'

'I've just been on the phone to the hospital,' Grey announced, tossing his mobile on to a desk. 'Toby Winchester is the real cheese, so it's just his father who's been switched.'

'I'm calling Huge Ego.' Highwater snatched up a phone without bothering to correct her slip.

Archie, Barney and Gemma waited while their boss explained STINKBOMB's theory to Hugh Figo, describing how Evelyn Tension and her two cohorts had deceived everyone and kidnapped the Prime Minister.

When Highwater had finished her spiel she listened in silence, nodding occasionally.

'Yes, sir,' she said at last. 'But . . . very well, sir . . . Yes, sir. Right away . . . Goodbye, sir.'

Highwater hung up and sighed deeply.

'What's the POA of action?' Holden Grey asked.

'I'm guessing Figo's going to invoke an immediate Code Three lockdown,' Barney suggested. 'They'll probably intercept Tension with two SBS patrol boats in a classic Stockholm Manoeuvre while Protocol Omega-Six should take care of the fake PM.'

'Isn't omega-six, like, a good bacteria or something?' Gemma murmured.

'For once, Agent Zulu, I wish you were right,'

Highwater said flatly. 'Because even though none of that makes any sense at all, it would be more useful than what Mr Ego is going to do.'

'Which is?' asked Archie.

'Nothing.'

'Nothing!?!' everyone chorused.

'Nothing.' Highwater shook her head wearily. 'He says our theory is pure fantasy and that he's not going to arrest the Prime Minister on the basis of a deranged schoolboy's sense of smell. He thinks it would make the Secret Service a laughing stock.'

'What about Malik?' Archie retorted angrily. 'How do they explain him being found drugged in his locker?'

'Malik was diagnosed as suffering from an acute case of post-traumatic stress – i.e. he was so terrified he was going to be in trouble for hurting Toby Winchester that he hid himself away in his locker. Apparently short-term memory loss is a common symptom of this kind of ordeal.'

'What about the fat suit and the wig?' Gemma demanded.

Highwater raised her palms. 'Evidence of some sort of prank but not a threat to national security, according to The Ego. In fact, he thinks the whole mission was a great success.'

Holden Grey gave a snort. 'He's too busy feathering his own cap to admit he might have dropped the ball in his own court.'

'That's as maybe.' Highwater pressed her fingertips on to her desktop. 'But as far as Figo and the rest of the world are concerned, the PM is alive and well and drinking tea with his cabinet as we speak. Evelyn Tension has achieved the perfect crime – one that nobody even knows has been committed.'

Chapter 23

Highwater's declaration was met with a pensive pause, which Gemma interrupted.

'Quick, put the TV on,' she instructed. 'According to the BBC website, the Prime Minister has just cut his cabinet meeting short to make a statement to the press.'

Highwater flicked the television on just in time to see someone identical to Adam Winchester positioning himself behind a bouquet of assorted microphones while scores of flashbulbs illuminated him. The impostor smiled grimly and held his hands up as he waited for the reporters' questions to cease.

'Boy, that's a great disguise,' Highwater marvelled. 'Maybe there really are two Adam Winchesters after all.'

Barney glanced curiously at Archie, who shook his head emphatically.

'As you know,' the man on the screen continued, 'I have just been in a meeting with my cabinet colleagues. During that meeting I shared with the ministers some information that came into my possession a few days ago.' The phoney Winchester pursed his lips and paused. 'I had hoped to deal with this matter via private diplomatic channels but I'm afraid the time has come for me to inform you, the British people, of the serious threat we are currently facing.' The PM's lookalike paused and made his lips go thin, as if he regretted being forced into disclosing the information. Inhaling through his nostrils, he continued with fresh resolve, 'I have in my possession a highly classified dossier detailing a secret nuclear weapons programme currently being undertaken in the very heart of Europe. The Swiss government has been using a chocolate factory as a front for a facility that is building and stockpiling nuclear weapons. According to my intelligence the famously neutral Swiss are planning to hold the rest of Europe to ransom. I have given them until midnight tonight to admit to their missile factory and shut it down or I will have no option but to respond in the strongest possible means.'

'What does that mean, Prime Minister?' called one journalist.

Adam Winchester flexed his jaw muscles, then with quiet menace said, 'It means I will order a nuclear air strike on Switzerland.'

As the crowd of reporters erupted, the fake Prime Minster held up a forefinger until the cacophony of shouted questions died away.

'I shall make no further comment until either the Swiss government complies with my terms or the deadline approaches,' the PM said sternly. 'Having taken the plunge I am in no doubt that this is the right course of action. While we await Switzerland's response I shall be deep in discussions with those around me. I concede this is a highly pressurised situation but rest assured I shall do everything in my power to fathom a solution and steer us into calmer waters. I promise we will emerge from this to find a new future in store for all of us.'

As the cameras whirred and journalists called out, the counterfeit Adam Winchester turned and went through the glossy black door of 10 Downing Street.

Highwater switched off the TV and scanned the pale faces in the room.

'OGM,' Grey uttered. 'It looks like Miss Tension is planning to start a nuclear war.'

'Will Switzerland nuke us back?' Archie asked.

'They don't really have nuclear warheads,' Highwater replied. 'But plenty of their allies do – and would be only too happy to fire on us. Then *our* allies would join in and before you know it we'd be in the middle of World War Three. But, unlike the first two, this one would have no survivors.'

'Surely the Prime Minister can't start a war on his own,' Barney said plaintively. 'I mean, he has to get the backing of the other dudes in his cabinet – right?'

'Most of them wouldn't want to stand up to him in case it hurt their careers,' Gemma muttered.

Archie ran his hand over his head, clutching a fistful of hair. 'Is there any chance someone will spot the PM's a fake?' he asked desperately.

'I thought he came across pretty smarmy,' Barney offered.

'I'm all over that, blood,' Grey agreed. 'He seemed phoney to me.'

'Definitely,' Archie said hopefully. 'In a way he was too polished – like he was obviously really well scripted.'

'Smarmy, phoney and well scripted,' Highwater

summarised. 'In other words he is *identical* to the real Adam Winchester.'

'Surely his family would realise he isn't the real deal?' said Archie.

'I hear you,' said Grey. 'Except Mrs Winchester is in Canada and Toby will be under observation in the hospital for twenty-four hours.'

Archie's phone began to vibrate and he answered it on the third ring. Before he could say a word he heard a voice say, 'Hello, Archie. This is Evelyn Tension.' Immediately all the colour drained from his cheeks. Jabbing a finger at the handset he mouthed two words to the others in the room – *It's her.* Turning the handset's loudspeaker on he said, 'How did you get my number?'

'Young man, I can assure you that getting your number was child's play for me.'

Highwater twirled a hand at Archie and nodded insistently. Gemma began tapping furiously at her keyboard.

'Uh . . . what are you up to?' Archie stuttered.

'Brave try, Archie,' Tension said sweetly. 'I think it's so cute that you want to play at being an agent and I know you want to impress your boss who's signalling you to keep me talking. But I'm not feeling playful today so listen up.'

'OK.'

'I'm sure, like me, you were shocked by the announcement Adam Winchester just made. It's so sad when countries fall out, isn't it? I mean, who would have suspected those nice neutral Swiss people of plotting something so . . . so despicable. If nothing is done I predict this will escalate to all-out nuclear war. Do you know what Armageddon is, Archie?'

'It means the end of the world,' Archie replied defiantly. 'But if you start a war that kills everyone, then who will ever know how brilliant you've been?'

'Oh, there'll be survivors,' Tension countered. 'Some tiny far flung mountain villages and remote islands will escape the fallout. Eventually the radiation will subside and the nuclear winter will pass and the world's population will start to grow again, slowly.' She lowered her voice to little more than a whisper. 'That's when I'll emerge from my shelter and reveal the despicable trick I've played on the world. Every child born in the post-apocalyptic age will grow up knowing about the sheer evil brought about by Evelyn Tension.'

'Why are you telling me?' Archie enquired. 'Shouldn't you call the real MI6?'

197

'Oh, they're so useless!' Tension snapped. 'It's no fun outsmarting them – it's too easy. They don't even know the PM's a phoney. You're a smart boy, Archie. I suspect you and your friends aren't too far behind me. If anyone can stop me destroying the world, it's you.'

'Keep her talking for ten more seconds,' Gemma whispered.

'Do you want us to stop you?' Archie asked.

'Darling, what a fascinating psychological question,' purred Tension. 'I could spend hours discussing my dreams with you. But time's up – goodbye.'

The line went dead and for a moment the room was quiet.

'No way!' Gemma growled, her fingers hammering her keyboard.

'What's the matter, X-ray?' Highwater enquired.

'I was trying to save the audio so we could at least prove to Figo what Tension is up to,' Gemma explained. 'But her voice pattern has some sort of anti-phase echo. It's like an audio shadow that exactly mirrors her words, effectively cancelling them out.'

'Meaning the tape is blank?'

Gemma shoved her keyboard away in frustration. 'Totally.'

Archie felt an air of despondency fill the room. He thought about his father and his grandmother and the millions of people who would perish if Tension's plan to destroy the world succeeded, and he experienced a profound sense of defiance.

'We can't let her win,' he said, gritting his teeth with determination.

'We have to expose the impostor,' Barney suggested. 'All we need to do is get close to the pretend PM, then rip his mask off.'

'Brilliant,' Gemma snorted sarcastically. 'I'm sure no one would mind if we wander into Number Ten and grab the Prime Minister's face.'

'I thought it was a good suggestion,' Archie said. Barney nodded his appreciation.

'It's not a *totally* ridiculous idea,' declared Highwater. 'But it is nevertheless impossible. The PM's bodyguards have orders to physically restrain anyone who tries to get within two metres of him. If you get too close they'll flatten you like a truck. Even I'm forbidden from crossing the two-metre line.'

'So how are we supposed to convince the world the dude in Number Ten is a fake?' asked Barney.

'Simple,' Archie replied, with a gleam in his eye. 'If

199

we can't expose the phoney PM, STINKBOMB will just have to find the real Adam Winchester and bring him back to London.'

'There's no way I can authorise you three to tackle Evelyn Tension alone,' Highwater said regretfully. 'You're fantastic agents – but you'll still need back-up to detain and bring in Tension. She is a trained assassin – an absolute monster.'

'What if we don't tackle her?' Archie pleaded. 'What if we track her using the Dragonfly? When we have her in sight you can send reinforcements to detain her and rescue the PM. If you tell Hugh Figo that Evelyn Tension or the PM has been *positively* identified then he'll have to respond.'

'So you wouldn't actually need to leave the plane?' Highwater clarified.

Archie shook his head. 'I can hover a few feet above the waves and head her off if she tries to escape.'

'And you promise not to board Tension's boat under any circumstance?'

Agents X-ray, Yankee and Zulu nodded earnestly.

'There's still one thing I don't understand,' said Highwater strictly. 'What on earth are you waiting for?'

Somewhere
Between
the O2 Arena and
Evelyn Tension's
Secret Hideout

Chapter 24

Evelyn Tension tilted her head to one side as she brushed her long copper-coloured hair. The computer screen in front of her flickered briefly, then showed a woman's face. She had straight black hair and almond-shaped eyes.

'Darling!' Tension exclaimed. 'How wonderful to see you. You look gorgeous in that uniform. That colour is so good on you.'

The woman glanced down at her yellow satin outfit and shrugged. 'You are the boss,' she replied robotically. 'We wear whatever you decide we wear.'

Evelyn Tension glanced across at Klaus, who was in the room with her. 'Did you hear that, Klausy?' she whispered. 'That's exactly the sort of respect I deserve, don't you think?'

Klaus dragged his mouth into a smile and nodded.

Turning back to the screen Tension said, 'Tell me, how are all my pussycats doing?'

'I assume you are referring to the other members of Cougar Squad. They are all engaged in their duties, as per your instructions.'

The woman on the screen stepped back to reveal a room crammed with mechanical equipment. Row upon row of gauges and dials lined the walls, and circular radar screens cast an eerie luminous glow across the scene. Three other women were sitting in front of radars, monitoring them closely, and two more were marching up and down, taking readings and making notes on their clipboards. All six of them were identically dressed in yellow satin jumpsuits, their dark hair slicked back.

Tension beamed and clapped her hands rapidly. 'I can't wait to see my girlies again. Have you all missed me?'

The woman's face filled the screen again. 'We have been busy fulfilling our duties, as instructed,' she replied flatly.

'Oh, I've missed you all too,' Tension oozed. Glancing at Klaus, she pressed her palms against her chest and mouthed the words *So adorable*.

'Do you have the package?' the woman demanded.

Tension looked at the man huddled at Klaus's feet. 'Oh yes,' she purred. 'Everything went like clockwork. We have the package and we'll be with you soon. There is a possibility some kids might be following us . . .'

'*Kids?*' The woman raised her eyebrows slightly. 'I'm sure we'll have no trouble eliminating *kids*.'

'Are you at the rendezvous point?' Tension enquired.

'Affirmative. We await your arrival.'

'I can't wait to see you too,' Tension enthused. 'Don't worry, I'll be home soon.'

The woman frowned. 'I am not worried.'

'That's my brave soldier,' Tension said softly. 'I promise when I get back we'll have some proper girly time. I need to catch up on all the gossip . . .' Her voice trailed off as she realised the woman had ended the call. She stared at the blank screen for a moment, her indulgent smile curdling slowly into a snarl. Spinning round to face Klaus, she yelled, 'Can't this thing go any faster? The sooner we get there the sooner we show this wretch what's in store for him.' One manicured talon extended towards the huddled figure. 'Then he'll rue the day he decided to double-cross Evelyn Tension.'

Chapter 25

Archie was first out of the O2 Arena's main entrance, clenching his teeth as he belted across the car park towards the Dragonfly. Gemma was close on his heels, her ponytail bouncing with each stride, and Barney brought up the rear, red-faced and wheezing.

By the time Barney reached the jet plane, Archie was already in the pilot's seat scanning the instruments and running through his checks. Barney clambered into the aircraft and squeezed behind the co-pilot's chair, slumping back into one of the two passenger seats. Gemma sat next to Archie and he slid the glass canopy forward and latched it closed.

Archie started the Dragonfly's two jet engines and applied maximum thrust. As the plane leaped into the air he eased it vertically upward a hundred feet before slamming the nozzle lever forward, launching the aircraft into the evening sky. He pulled the stick back, and to the right, and the Dragonfly banked steeply as it climbed away, heading towards the mouth of the Thames and the open sea beyond.

Gemma was tapping away on the foldout keyboard of the newly installed Mode Foxtrot comms kit, using the screen in front of her to display the satellite images she was accessing.

'We're nearly at the coast,' Archie said. 'I'll need a direction to fly when we get there.'

'Hold your horses,' Gemma murmured, squinting at the screen. 'I'm tracking them down the river by leapfrogging CCTV footage. I've got them at the coast at two-fifteen but then they go out of range of ground-based cameras. I just need to find which satellite was covering the Thames estuary at that time.'

Barney leaned eagerly between the front seats. 'Have you tried feeding the coordinates into the NASA Geomotionary Orbital Matrices? Then it's simply a matter of pinpointing the exact moment on the theoretical quasi-elliptical time-phase axis – right?'

'I haven't got time for this, Zulu.' Gemma turned

and glared at Barney. 'I'll send *you* into orbit if you don't pipe down.'

Archie glanced over his shoulder at Barney, who looked chastened. 'He's only trying to help, X-ray,' he said.

'Sorry,' Gemma sighed.

Barney slumped back into his seat and stared out the window, mumbling under his breath, 'I suppose everything else Jack Bauer said was made up as well then, was it?'

'Bingo!' Gemma yelped. 'I've picked them up on the Sierra-16 satellite. The footage was taken at fourteen-twelve and shows them heading north-east.'

Archie glanced at the plane's digital clock. 'They're four hours ahead of us. Can you see how fast they were going?'

Gemma tapped a few keys. 'Man, they're blitzing at nearly a hundred knots.'

'They must be in some kind of jet boat,' said Archie, checking the Dragonfly's airspeed. 'It's going to take us about an hour to catch up with them.'

The Dragonfly ripped through the sky, just five hundred feet above the inky water. Archie kept the controls at his fingertips, easing the stick fractionally one way or another to keep the plane on a level course. Meanwhile Gemma's fingers were dancing over her keyboard.

'Oh, man!' she exclaimed.

'What's up?' Archie asked.

'Well, the S-16 satellite was redirected at ten past four,' Gemma explained. 'MI5 or 6 must be tracking some security threat of some kind.'

'Probably a Daedalus Nine Alert or something,' Barney whispered – more to himself than the others.

'So we've lost them?' Archie said, feeling suddenly desperate.

'We *had* . . .' Gemma smiled. 'Until I accessed the global satellite mapping data files and picked them up a few minutes later on the Saturn-7 camera which just so happened to be overlapping the S-16 coverage. The chances of that happening are, like, almost zero.'

'But what happens if Saturn-7 is redirected as well?'

'It can't be.' Gemma glanced at Archie triumphantly. 'I've accessed the satellite's control functions via the Mode Foxtrot kit.'

Archie's eyebrows climbed his forehead as Gemma's words registered. 'So you're actually controlling a real-life satellite?'

'Totally!' Gemma whooped. 'I am all over them with Saturn-7. There's no way Tension can escape us now.'

An hour later the Dragonfly was tearing through the night sky over the North Sea, about fifty miles south-west of the Danish coast. Gemma had kept the Saturn-7 satellite trained on the fleeing powerboat, logging its coordinates every five minutes and passing them to Archie who programmed them into the plane's navigation computer.

'They're only ten miles ahead of us,' Archie said. 'So we should see them in a couple of minutes.'

'If Saturn-7 didn't have infra-red thermal imaging we'd never have caught them,' Gemma commented.

'We haven't caught them yet,' Archie cautioned, studying the black void ahead.

'What's that?' Gemma yelped, pointing. 'Just to the right of the nose!'

In the moonlight something was casting a lozenge-shaped shadow on the water, skipping noiselessly as it retreated over the waves.

'It's them,' Archie confirmed, squinting into the night. 'I'm going to drop down in front of the boat and head them off.'

210

As the Dragonfly cruised past the speedboat, Archie held his course for thirty seconds, outrunning the boat by about two miles, then snapped the nozzle-control lever back to the 'hover' gate. As the plane's forward speed died its three occupants lurched forward against their harnesses. Spinning the aircraft with a kick of the rudder pedals, Archie pulled back the power and allowed the Dragonfly to descend until it was just a few feet above the icy sea.

Archie watched the powerboat emerging from the night as it raced towards them.

'Er . . . they don't appear to be slowing down,' Barney observed.

'That's because they can't see us,' Archie replied. 'Let me know when they're half a mile away, X-ray. Then I'll throw on our landing lights and give them the fright of their lives.'

'You got it.'

Bouncing rhythmically, the boat speared towards them like an Exocet missile.

'They're coming up *really* fast,' Barney whispered.

'Patience,' Archie murmured, reaching up and hooking two fingers over the Dragonfly's landing-light switches.

The boat sped nearer.

'But I mean *seriously* fast,' Barney insisted.

'Not yet,' Archie breathed.

'OK, on the count of three,' said Gemma. 'One . . . two . . . three . . . now!'

As Archie flicked the two switches to illuminate the Dragonfly, a terrific explosion ripped a hole in the night and a massive fireball engulfed the entire plane.

Chapter 26

For a moment the three agents held their breath as the black cloud swallowed their plane. Instinctively Archie slammed on full power and hauled the control column back, driving the Dragonfly up and backwards, rocking violently with the force of the blast.

'We're toast!' Barney cried.

Suddenly the plane was thrown out of the fireball, like a rock being spat from an erupting volcano. Archie fought with his controls as the Dragonfly arced backwards, violently rolling – threatening to flip over. Just managing to control the plane, Archie eased the aircraft into a descent, returning to just above sea level in order to inspect Tension's speedboat. But there was nothing to inspect. Where the boat had once been there was nothing but open water, littered with shreds of smoking debris. Pieces of flaming wreckage were still raining on to the water like matchsticks.

'What about the Prime Minister?' asked Gemma helplessly.

'Dead,' Archie snapped in despair. 'They're all dead. No one could've survived that explosion.'

'What are we going to do?' asked Barney, absently opening a Twix to calm his nerves.

'There's nothing we can do,' Archie answered quietly. 'We have to go home.'

'But we can't just leave the PM here,' Gemma argued.

'Well, we certainly can't take him with us,' Archie retorted. 'Unless you've got a sieve handy to strain the whole ocean?'

Archie and Gemma glared angrily at each other.

'OK, guys,' Barney said calmly, poking his head between the two front seats. 'We're all upset but let's try and chill out, yeah?'

'Great.' Gemma craned her neck and smiled sarcastically at Barney. 'The Prime Minister's been killed by a suicidal villain, who has replaced him with an evil lookalike intent on leading us into World War Three, but you think we should all *chill out*?'

214

Barney's cheeks coloured and he smiled nervously.

Archie interjected. 'He's just saying we ought to try to keep calm and cool off.'

'Cool off?!' Gemma repeated. 'The only way I could cool off right now is if I jumped head first into the freezing sea beneath us – and I am certainly not about to take the plunge! So, if you haven't got anything useful to say, don't say anything at all!'

Barney nodded vigorously.

Gemma looked at Archie, who was staring at the horizon – instinctively controlling the plane's hover. His mind was racing and, as the thoughts flashed through his head, a knowing grin tugged at the corners of his mouth.

'What's there to smile about?' Gemma demanded.

'Gemma – you're an absolute genius,' he said excitedly. 'What you just said has given me a totally wicked idea.'

'For the record,' Barney piped up, 'what Gemma just said was in direct response to my delicate provocation. I was deliberately goading her into saying . . . whatever it was that was so brilliant.'

'OK!' Archie laughed. 'You're both brilliant.'

'Are you going to tell us why?' Gemma enquired.

Archie nodded. 'You just said you were not going to "take the plunge" – which is exactly the phrase the sham Adam Winchester used in his statement.'

'So?' Gemma shrugged. 'It's just a figure of speech?'

'I know,' Archie agreed, his eyes shining keenly behind his rectangular specs. 'He also said he would be *deep* in discussions and that this was a highly *pressurised* situation.'

'OK, you've got a good *memory*,' Gemma conceded. 'But why are you *stressing* random *words*?'

'They're not random. I think Tension was taunting us with her henchman's statement. She was using the fake PM to tell us where she was taking the real one. Think about it,' Archie urged. 'They've taken the *plunge* and now they're *deep* in a *highly pressurised* situation.'

Barney gasped and his eyes widened. 'A submarine!' he exclaimed.

'Exactly,' Archie confirmed.

'O-M-G, you're right,' Gemma said. 'And he said he was going to *fathom* a solution and something about *emerging* into *calmer waters*. It's so obvious now, I can't believe we didn't spot it at the time. But why give us any clues at all?'

'Criminal masterminds have to show off about

216

how brilliant they are, and how thick everyone else is,' Barney said. 'It's the law.'

'X-ray, check the satellite footage,' Archie instructed. 'They must have jumped overboard before detonating the bomb on their boat.'

Gemma's keyboard was purring instantly. 'OK, I've zoomed in on the powerboat and I'm rewinding it from the time of the explosion.'

Archie's pulse was sky high. If he was wrong about Tension diving overboard then all was lost. There would be no way of stopping Adam Winchester's impostor leading the world into nuclear war. He glanced at the Dragonfly's clock. It was already eight fifteen in the evening. Only three hours and forty-five minutes remained until the fake PM would order the nuclear air strike.

'Score!' shouted Gemma.

The grainy image on her computer screen showed a dark silhouette of a speedboat. Gemma pointed to a tiny black speck behind the boat. 'There's our first man overboard.' She tapped a key and the video began to play. Almost simultaneously two more dark spots appeared at the back of the boat. 'And there's the other two.'

'Looks like they jumped ship just before we overtook them,' Barney observed.

'Which means Tension still doesn't know how close we are,' Archie mused. 'What time did they hit the water?'

'Exactly eight minutes ago,' said Gemma.

'I'll RV with IC and send her the drop-zone coordinates,' Barney suggested, tapping the screen on his spiPhone. 'She'll need to scramble the SBS pronto.'

'There's no time for that,' Archie argued, flying the Dragonfly towards the position where the boat's occupants had entered the sea. 'By the time Special Forces get here, Tension's submarine could be miles away and leagues under the sea. She might be impossible to track down again. The only way we have a chance of catching her and saving the PM is to board the sub ourselves, immediately.'

'Wait,' Gemma protested, leaning involuntarily forward as the plane lurched to a hover. 'STINKBOMB's orders were to locate and contain the speedboat. We promised IC that we would not go after Tension.'

'Actually we only promised her we wouldn't board Tension's speedboat,' Archie said, throwing the switch marked ATLAS and dropping the undercarriage lever.

'Nobody said anything about sneaking on to her submarine and rescuing the PM.'

The plane jolted as its floats hit the sea with a slap and Archie killed the engines. It was suddenly eerily quiet as the Dragonfly bobbed gently on the water.

'Agent Yankee makes an excellent point,' Barney commented, opening the hatch behind him and reaching in.

'OK, let's go,' said Archie, taking the Scuba gear Barney was passing to him.

'Wait!' Gemma barked. '*I* am the senior agent on this assignment so *I* decide our next move. And there's no way we're going to jump straight into the sea and dive underwater in search of some evil villain's submarine.'

Archie paused, his wetsuit rucked up as far as his knees. Barney's eyes were agog behind his mask.

After a beat the corners of Gemma's mouth twitched. '*First* we're going to weigh anchor so the Dragonfly doesn't float away,' she said sternly. '*Then* we're going to jump in and get aboard that evil villain's submarine. Looks like STINKBOMB's going to have to save the world. Again!'

Chapter 27

Archie pulled the full-face diving mask over his head. The rubber balaclava was fitted with a bulbous perspex visor that encompassed his face from forehead to chin. A tube fed oxygen from a tank on his back through a regulator valve attached to the outside of the mask, under his chin. Archie could breathe the air supply inside his mask without having to suck on a mouthpiece, so he was able to talk freely. The three agents had inserted earpieces fitted with tiny microphones to allow them to maintain two-way communications under water.

'Good luck, STINKBOMB,' Archie said with a brave smile.

'Good luck,' Barney and Gemma chorused back.

'Wait!' Barney piped up. 'When we rescue the PM

220

aren't we going to need a wetsuit for him? There's only three in the hatch.'

'We'll deal with that when the time comes,' Archie suggested. 'Right now our priority is finding Adam Winchester.'

He climbed on to the edge of the cockpit, placed one hand over his face mask and stepped into thin air. As well as the wetsuit, he was wearing neoprene gloves and boots but as he plunged into the sea the icy water rushed under the rubber and took his breath away. Kicking his feet, he punched back through the surface, gasping air.

'Come on in!' he called up to the others. 'The water's lovely.'

'If you're a polar bear, maybe,' Gemma replied.

Archie heard two heavy splashes and a moment later Barney and Gemma were bobbing next to him, gasping and thrashing about.

He gave them a few moments to catch their breath, then said, 'OK, let's see if we can find that submarine. Stay close together – I'll go first.'

'OK,' Gemma replied.

'Copy that,' said Barney. 'I hear you loud and clear. It's feeding time for the penguin but the blue whale has eaten all the crabs.'

'Let's try and keep the comms to a minimum,' Archie suggested. 'Follow me.' He ducked his head into the water, his feet appeared briefly, then he slipped down and out of sight. Gemma followed his lead, then Barney rolled his eyes in dismay before diving below the surface.

The masks they were wearing had strips of high power LED lights fitted in the seal, but soon even the specialised head-torches penetrated little more than a yard into the eternal blackness as the agents swam deeper.

The only sound Archie heard was the rhythmic rush of his own breathing. Air bubbles flashed briefly in the light before being swallowed by the ocean. He quickly felt disorientated – dangerously exposed to the immense power of the sea and vulnerable to whatever creatures lurked below.

Archie turned his head left and right, straining his eyes for a glimpse of any distant clue that Evelyn Tension might be in the vicinity. Sensing something skulking in the gloom ahead, he grabbed Gemma's arm. As the agents drifted tentatively forward, transfixed by the shadowy form, it emerged into an enormous torpedo-shaped vessel.

'Whoa!' Gemma exclaimed, treading water

furiously. 'A submarine.'

'A Russian Typhoon-class sub, to be precise,' Barney whispered.

'It's got to be Tension's lair,' Archie stated, a squirt of adrenalin quickening his pulse. 'Wait here – I'm going to check it out.'

With his hands by his sides and his belly close to the surface of the huge metal vessel, he followed the contours of its rounded nose. The body of the submarine swelled, before tapering along its considerable length to a narrow tail. Archie turned and swam back to his friends, this time scanning the hull's belly.

'It's huge,' he reported, bobbing opposite Barney and Gemma. 'At least thirty metres long and it's a really weird shape.'

'In what way?' Gemma enquired.

'Well, it's got a big dorsal fin on its back and flippers on each side,' Archie explained, a trail of bubbles pouring out of his regulator. 'And its rear end splays out like a fish tail. I think it's been customised to look like some sort of whale.'

'Boy, is she evil,' Barney said knowingly.

'Care to explain?' Gemma sighed.

'Dolphins swim with whales!' Barney exclaimed.

'Obviously Tension lures the dolphins close to her sub, then grabs them with some sort of giant mechanical grabber-thingy that pops out from somewhere, and pulls them aboard to feed to her crew.'

'Obviously,' Archie said quietly. 'Or maybe it's shaped like this so it will just look like a whale on any passing ship's sonar?'

Barney swallowed audibly. 'That's another theory, I suppose.'

'I think the more pressing question is "How are we going to get inside?"' Gemma said.

'I think I know,' Archie said with a grin. 'This way.'

He led the others over the top of the steel whale's nose to a position high on the centre of its head where a stubby cylinder stuck out from the sleek profile like a turret. The protrusion was two metres in diameter and one metre high, its flat surface adorned with a cross-shaped locking handle.

'Let me guess,' Gemma sneered. 'We just turn the lock and jump in – simple as?'

'Got any better ideas?' Archie retorted.

Gripping two opposite ends of the handle, he heaved with all his strength, trying to twist it anticlockwise. It didn't budge.

'Yankee, you pull this end,' Archie instructed. 'I'll push this one.'

Both boys strained against the mechanism but still it wouldn't move.

'Oh, for heaven's sake, let me have a go,' Gemma said impatiently. Gritting her teeth, she tried to lever the handle free. With a sudden clunk the lock rotated ninety degrees and Gemma turned to her fellow agents, smiling smugly.

'We must have loosened it for you,' said Archie.

Gemma spun the handle freely and four holes sprang open on the circular hatch. Seawater poured through the holes and hammered against the steel compartment inside.

A moment later the portal opened automatically, like a clamshell, revealing a metal capsule three metres deep that was now filled with seawater.

'It's a floodable airlock – like a safety-valve,' Archie explained. 'We have to climb inside and close the door again. When the outer door is locked, the water in the capsule will be pumped overboard – then we can open the inner door.'

The three agents manoeuvred themselves feet first into the cylindrical capsule and pulled the hatch shut above their heads. As the levers clunked into position the four holes in the door closed and an immense slurping noise echoed round the capsule.

'I feel like I'm inside a washing machine,' said Gemma as the water gushed around her.

'That explains why you're so shirty,' Barney mumbled.

'Come on, Agent Zulu.' Archie smiled. 'Stop being such a big girl's blouse.'

Suddenly the water level in the capsule began to drop rapidly. Within seconds Archie, Barney and Gemma were lowered on to the floor of the compartment and after a minute they were surrounded by warm, dry air.

Archie tentatively removed his mask. Sensing the atmosphere contained plenty of oxygen he gave the others a thumbs-up signal and they removed their headgear too. They all placed their equipment inside a recess in the wall and surveyed their surroundings.

The metal cylinder had a single rectangular door locked with a familiar cross-shaped handle.

'So we go through that door and we're inside Tension's sub?' Archie surmised.

'Does anyone else get the feeling this has all been a bit too easy?' questioned Barney.

'Easy? You can talk,' said Gemma drily. 'If I hadn't

226

been here you two would still be struggling to open the hatch.'

Archie grinned. 'Good point.'

'If this was a trap the intruder sirens would be going crazy by now,' Barney advised. 'There'd be flashing lights and guards all over us.'

Archie grabbed the door handle, heaving it anticlockwise. There was a satisfying metallic clunk as the door unlocked. He listened for a moment.

Silence.

'So far so good,' he whispered, easing the door open an inch.

That was when the almighty wail of an air-raid siren screamed through the cramped compartment.

'So much for sneaking in under the radar!' Archie yelled, trying to make himself heard above the racket.

'They might not know where the alarm was raised!' Barney shouted back. 'If they knew we were here there'd be loads of guards waiting for us.'

Gemma nodded resolutely. 'So it could be worse.'

Archie pushed the metal hatch open another inch and peered through the crack. Closing the door and locking it again, he turned to Barney and Gemma. 'Actually,' he said calmly, 'It *really* couldn't be any worse.'

227

Chapter 28

'There are six guards heading this way,' Archie advised the others. 'Anybody got any ideas?'

'We could unlock the outer hatch,' Gemma suggested. 'The whole point of the two-stage entry system is that only one door can be opened at any time. If they override it the whole sub would be flooded.'

'True.' Archie nodded. 'But then the PM would be trapped here indefinitely.'

'I think you mean *definitely*, dude,' Barney said. 'I mean, there's no doubt he'd be trapped.'

'No, I meant . . .' Archie sighed. 'OK. Good point.'

Barney shrugged modestly. 'I say we go out there and kick some butt.'

'Kick butt?' Gemma exclaimed with exaggerated

surprise. 'No Code Orpheus protocol or Level Unicorn alert?'

'Zulu,' Archie said, as though waking him from a dream. 'We're outnumbered two to one. And to be fair, you're not exactly much use in a fight – no offence – and X-ray's more of a hacker than a whacker. There's no way I can beat six of them.'

Suddenly there was hammering on the door and someone yelled, '*Come out now. We know you're in there.*'

'Just a minute,' Archie called brightly as though he was taking his time in the bathroom.

'It doesn't matter that you're outnumbered,' Barney whispered. 'Guards in an evil mastermind's hideout only ever attack one at a time. Everyone knows that.'

Gemma and Archie exchanged sceptical glances.

'*If you're not out here on three – we're coming in to get you. One . . . two . . .*'

In one swift movement Archie turned the handle and rammed the door open, feeling it jar as it struck something solid outside. As the hatch swung open he was faced with six guards, lined up single-file along a narrow walkway. The one at the front was writhing in agony, face in hands.

'Ooops. Did I get you with the door?' Archie winced

apologetically. 'Sorry, I thought you said *three*.'

As Archie spoke the injured guard staggered backwards and toppled over the waist-high railing. There was a moment's silence, then the distant whump of a body hitting the deck below.

'And then there were five,' Archie muttered.

The remaining guards raised their fists, ready for combat. They were all wearing yellow satin jumpsuits and black lipstick, and sporting a straight fringe and a ponytail.

'Evening, ladies,' said Gemma, following Archie out of the hatch. 'I can see how embarrassing this must be for you all. It's bad enough when you turn up somewhere and find *one* other person wearing the same outfit . . .'

'We do not concern ourselves with frivolities such as fashion,' snarled one guard.

'So I see,' Gemma mumbled. 'I mean, those jumpsuits aren't doing anyone any favours.'

'Silence!' snapped the guard. 'You are our prisoners now. We will take you to our leader who will decide your fate. Handcuff them!'

As a guard approached Archie he dropped into a wide-legged combat stance. 'Stay behind me,' he whispered to the others.

The female guard stalked towards him, suddenly throwing a straight punch at his face. Blocking the blow, Archie snapped out a fist that struck his opponent in the stomach, doubling her over. Grabbing her ankles he hoisted her over the railing, then turned to face the next guard, who was waiting to attack.

This one launched a roundhouse kick that Archie ducked before sweeping away her standing foot with his leg. As the female guard crashed on to the metal walkway he rolled her under the railing, listening for the imminent whump.

The next guard charged immediately, landing a punch on Archie's cheek before he could react. As he reeled backwards the guard followed up with another punch. Recovering quickly, Archie grabbed her wrist, rocked backwards and sat down. He pressed the sole of his foot into her stomach and tossed her over his head before jumping up to face his next battle.

He dispatched guard number five with a spinning kick that connected with her shoulder and sent her sprawling over the edge of the gangway.

The last guard attacked with a flurry of punches, striking Archie square on the nose and snapping his head back. Shaking off the blow, he noticed, behind the guard, a hole in the gangway fitted with a metal ladder leading to the sub's lower level. Sensing an opportunity, he responded with a barrage of his own, forcing her back along the walkway with stiff blows to her body.

Just a metre before the hole the guard seemed to recover her composure and stood her ground, squaring up to Archie. Maintaining his momentum, he skipped on to his left foot, driving out his right leg like a piston and striking her square in the chest. With a breathless groan she stumbled backwards, unable to stop herself stepping into the hole, and disappeared from view.

Archie glanced through the hole to see the guard slumped on the gloomy deck below.

Shaking his head, he muttered, 'What a dropout.'

But when he turned to give Barney and Gemma the all-clear his sense of victory turned instantly to cold terror.

The guard he had thrown over his shoulder had recovered and was sneaking up behind Barney. Her right hand – raised above her head – was holding a long curved knife, which she was about to bring down into his back.

'Look out!' Archie yelled.

Barney spun round, freezing in terror at the sight of his would-be assassin wielding her weapon.

With deadly intent the guard swung the knife downward. A full five metres away, Archie watched helplessly as the knife flashed towards his friend.

Gemma acted instantly – shoulder-barging Barney out of the knife's path.

As the blade now slashed down at her own face Gemma flicked out a hand, catching the guard's wrist and twisting it back. The female assassin swung her free fist angrily but Gemma's reactions were quicker. Blocking her opponent's blow with her forearm, Gemma landed a punch on the guard's chin, sending her reeling on to the deck and rolling over the edge of the gangway.

Barney scratched his tight blond curls and shook his head in bewilderment. 'You . . . you saved my life. Thank you, X-ray.'

'You're welcome.' Gemma shrugged, smiling briefly. 'But I won't be bragging about it and I think it's better for both our reputations if no one finds out. Ever.'

Barney nodded once. 'Consider it a code Six Quebec incident.'

'Whatever.' Gemma shrugged.

233

'That was awesome, Agent X-ray,' Archie enthused, arriving on the scene. 'I had no idea you were combat trained.'

'I'm not just a pretty face you know,' Gemma mumbled.

'No, you're not,' Archie said emphatically. 'What I mean is that you're *more* than just a pretty face. I didn't mean *No, you're not pretty* because clearly you are . . . very pretty.' Archie could feel his mouth drying up and his throat tightening. 'Isn't she, Zulu?'

Barney just grinned at Archie, whose face was turning a deep plum colour.

The awkward silence was interrupted by a female voice crackling from one of the guard's walkie-talkies that was lying on the walkway.

'Cougar Squad, this is Queen Bee, do you read? Do we have a code nine? I repeat, do we have a code nine?'

Archie, Barney and Gemma stared at the radio for a moment, then Barney picked it up and slowly raised it to his mouth.

'Keep it simple,' Gemma whispered.

Clearing his throat, Barney pressed the transmit switch and, in a high-pitched voice, replied, 'Queen

Bee, from Cougar Squad. Negative on the code nine. I repeat, negative. Over.'

The STINKBOMB agents held their breath and waited to hear if Barney's ruse had worked. After a few seconds the response crackled through the radio.

'Roger that, Cougar Squad. Stand down and return to the Command Deck.'

Archie exhaled loudly and Gemma nodded, both relieved that their cover hadn't been blown. Then Barney pressed the transmit button on the walkie-talkie again. 'Copy that and roger wilco,' he squeaked. 'I think it must have been a false alarm – probably a level three breach caused by some sort of hydroplutonic power surge in the . . . er . . . flux capacitor.'

Archie was shaking his head frantically while Gemma made furious cutting gestures across her throat – but Barney continued.

'We've checked the sector-six perimeter and we'll conduct a sweep of the alpha-nine modules, then RV at the Command Deck. Over.'

'Cougar Squad, your last transmission was garbled. Did you say a *hydroplutonic* power surge?'

Before Barney could say any more, Archie snatched the radio from his hand and tossed it over the railing – giving a nod of finality when he heard it shatter on impact.

'What did you do that for?' Barney complained.

'It slipped,' Archie lied. 'Sorry.'

'Shame,' Gemma added. 'And you were doing such a good job of keeping it simple too.'

'We'd better get moving,' Archie urged. 'The Command Deck is bound to be near the front of the sub. Come on.'

Archie turned and jogged along the metal gangway, hurdling the manhole the sixth guard had fallen through. Gemma followed, skipping over the void, while Barney stepped gingerly across, nervously gripping both handrails.

A short distance along the gloomy corridor they came to a closed doorway in a wall of solid steel. Unscrewing the handle, Archie opened the hatch and ducked through tentatively.

He found himself on another metal gangway leading through a compartment crammed with machinery and pipes. A ladder through a manhole disappeared into the gloom both above and below.

'This place seems much bigger than I thought it was,' Archie sighed.

'That's pretty standard.' Barney nodded wisely. 'Odious masterminds' hideouts often look pretty small from the outside but actually seem to go on forever on the inside.'

'OK, let's split up,' Archie suggested. 'I'll take the ladder up. Zulu, you investigate this level, and X-ray, you climb down to the level below. Meet back here in five minutes . . . unless one of us finds what we're looking for. Stay in touch.' Archie tapped his earpiece and the other two agents nodded.

Archie climbed ten rungs and clambered through a hole on to another gangway. The walls of the cramped corridor were also lined with networks of intertwined pipes, festooned with valves and pressure gauges. Every so often a jet of steam would puncture the eerie silence with a spiteful hiss.

Archie was beginning to feel claustrophobic. He felt an immense desire to see the sky and the sun and spread his arms wide. Staring along the walkway, he felt as if the walls were going to press together, squashing him flat.

Seeing no more guards, he forced himself to head towards the middle of the ship. He was conscious of his footsteps clanging on the metal gangway but he knew the time for stealth had passed. He reckoned Tension would probably have grown suspicious about her missing henchwomen by now, and was probably monitoring him on her CCTV.

Regardless of whether Evelyn Tension was aware of his presence or not, he had to rescue Adam Winchester and expose the fake PM before the midnight deadline, and to achieve that he had to move fast. Alerting her to STINKBOMB's presence was a risk he had to take.

Through an open hatch he found a long compartment crammed with bunks stacked three high and end to end. The only privacy afforded in the sleeping quarters was a curtain across each bed. As he edged along the narrow corridor between the bunks Archie noticed that the curtain on the far-right bed on the top level was drawn shut.

Trying not to make a sound, he crept along until he was next to the bed. Taking a quiet, deep breath he reached out and pinched the edge of the curtain between his fingers. Unsure whether he was about to come face to face with another murderous guard or a terrified Prime Minister, he steeled himself for action.

With a flick of his wrist he snapped the curtain back.

He gasped.

The bed was empty.

With his heart still hammering, Archie started making his way back to the ladder he'd just climbed.

'STINKBOMB, this is Yankee,' he murmured. 'Nothing but sleeping quarters on the top level. *Empty* sleeping quarters.'

'This is Zulu. The middle level leads deep into the engine room. The eagle has left the henhouse. We have a code green situation and a negative on Darth Vader. Over.'

'Come in, X-ray,' Archie ordered, climbing on to the top rung of the ladder. 'What's your position?'

Archie paused as he waited for Gemma's response.

Silence.

'X-ray, this is Yankee. Do you copy?'

Again there was silence, then . . .

'This is X-ray.' Gemma sounded shaken, breathless. 'Get down here now! I'm fifteen metres in front of the ladder. Stay low as you approach. I'm hiding behind a steel cylinder on the right of the gangway – and you are not going to *believe* what I've found.'

239

Chapter 29

Lightly gripping the ladder's vertical stringers, Archie slid down like a fireman descending a pole and dropped through the hole in the middle level.

Landing lightly at the foot of the ladder, Archie crouched low and ran towards the front of the submarine. After a short distance he was approaching an open hatch in a solid steel bulkhead when he spotted a large metal cylinder to his right and, in the half-light, a figure crouching behind it.

He scurried over and sat next to Gemma, resting his back against the giant drum.

'Where's Zulu?' she asked.

'He's coming, I think,' Archie replied, adjusting his spectacles. 'Speak of the devil.'

Grunting and puffing, Barney was crawling along the floor on his elbows and knees. When he was level with the others, he rolled sideways towards them. Unfortunately he tumbled with too much vigour and his head hit the cylinder with a resounding clang.

'What's going down?' he asked, rubbing his brow as he dragged himself up on to his knees.

'Our chances of staying undercover after your arrival,' Gemma muttered. She turned and peeked around the side of the steel drum. 'Check it out,' she said, jerking her head.

Archie and Barney peered cautiously through the open hatch and took in the scene that lay beyond.

'So this is where the Queen Bee spins her evil web,' Barney whispered.

Wide-eyed, Archie nodded. 'I couldn't have put it better myself.'

The walls of the circular room through the hatch were lined with steel panels containing knobs, levers, switches, dials and countless computer screens. The luminous green lines sweeping around numerous radar displays filled the air with an eerie glow.

Archie realised the two circular portholes, on opposite sides of the room, were designed to look like whale's

241

eyes from outside the sub. The telescopic column of the periscope reached from the floor to the domed ceiling, disappearing through the whale's blowhole. Archie gasped as his eyes fixed on the terrifying scene in the middle of the room. Raised about a metre from the deck was a circular platform measuring three metres across. It was surrounded by a trench that was two metres wide and brimming with a bubbling turquoise fluid, like a toxic moat. A man, wearing a guard's yellow jumpsuit, was spreadeagled on the round island and his wrists and ankles were clamped firmly down with steel manacles. He appeared to be conscious but a restraint around his neck gave him only limited movement of his head.

Suspended above the mini-stage was a large futuristic cannon. On top of its bulbous silver casing was a glass capsule containing a fluorescent orange liquid. The huge gun was tilted downward, shooting a single narrow beam of intense red light at the platform. Fizzing and hissing, it was scorching the metal, edging its way torturously between the prisoner's legs.

Even though the captive's nose and mouth were covered by a square of aluminium duct tape, and one of his eyes was bruised and swollen, Archie knew instantly who he was.

'It's Adam Winchester,' he said in a barely audible whisper, his heart pumping fast.

'Judging by his black eye he put up quite a struggle,' Gemma noted.

'It looks like Darth Vader is going to be on the wrong end of that light sabre if we don't do something,' said Barney.

'Let's just go in and get him,' Gemma suggested.

'We'd never get over that moat,' Archie said. 'I don't know what that liquid is but it's bound to be poisonous.'

'Or violently acidic, or swarming with piranha fish,' Barney suggested. 'Oooh – or it might contain some sort of truth serum designed to make us give up state secrets . . .'

'The state secret I want answered is who stole your brain,' Gemma murmured.

Archie knelt down, ducking his head low to the floor so that he could see the ceiling of the Command Room.

About three metres off the ground a thick steel strut was suspended horizontally. One end was connected to a heavy-duty steel hinge that was bolted to the roof, while the free end supported a segment of metal walkway. The arrangement reminded Archie of a strange fairground ride, frozen at the height of its swing. He calculated that if the strut swung down into the vertical position, the segment of walkway would span the moat round the island.

'It looks like Tension's engineered an elaborate drawbridge,' he commented, nodding at the ramp. 'There must be a control panel somewhere to lower it into position.'

'I suppose it would have been too easy to, like, slide a plank of wood across the gap or something,' Gemma sneered.

'But she is a *true* Evil Genius,' Barney whispered with a hint of admiration. 'In my experience of these people they *never* miss an opportunity to install some needlessly complicated mechanical contraptions.'

'Remind me,' Gemma muttered. 'How many Odious Masterminds have you actually met?'

'Doctor Doom,' Barney answered, sticking a thumb up as if he was about to count off a long list on his fingers. He rolled his eyes skyward and bit his lip.

Gemma snorted derisorily. 'Hang on, let me add them up . . . One.'

'That's still one more than you, if I'm not mistaken?' Barney retorted.

'That's a very good point,' Archie chuckled.

244

Gemma narrowed her eyes and smiled sarcastically.

'OK, let's concentrate on the matter in hand,' Archie said firmly.

'I say we go into the room and check it out,' Gemma replied. 'If we can find the controls for that bridge and unlock those manacles we might be able to get the PM out of there before anyone else even turns up.'

Archie considered the plan for a moment, then deciding it was about their only option, said, 'OK. Let's go.'

'Wait!' Barney gripped Archie's arm urgently. 'We need a go code.'

'A go code?' Archie repeated.

'Yeah. It's a secret phrase that tells your fellow agents that a mission is about to go live.'

'Listen.' Gemma fixed Barney with a hard stare. 'We don't have time for all your Hollywood jargon. You're starting to really wind me up.'

'It's a teensy bit *wordy*,' Barney said. 'How about we just use the last bit?'

With a frustrated groan Gemma turned and ducked through the hatch into the Command Room. Archie went in behind her, then Barney hoisted himself to his feet and stepped through the doorway, muttering,

245

'You're starting to really wind me up. Copy all units, *You're starting to really wind me up.*'

Archie turned as he walked into the Command Room, scanning the banks of control panels for something that might control the drawbridge. Gemma went straight to the bubbling blue moat surrounding Adam Winchester's podium. Barney tiptoed in, unwrapping a Mars – one of five chocolate bars he had stashed inside his wetsuit.

'We'll never get across without the bridge,' Gemma said, sizing up the chasm between her and the PM's raised platform. Glancing up at Adam Winchester, she added, 'Don't worry your . . . excellence, sir, we'll get you out of here.'

The Prime Minister's desperate pleas were muffled by the tape over his mouth.

As Archie studied the mass of switches and levers on the walls he felt his eyes straining. Finding the correct control panel was like looking for a needle in a haystack. Meanwhile Barney was staring at an area of the wall immediately to the right of the hatch they had come through.

'Check this out,' he said idly, chomping away another inch of his Mars bar.

246

'Not now, Zulu,' Archie replied tetchily, sweeping his eyes down a panel swimming with row upon row of tiny circuit breakers. 'We need to find the control for the bridge before Tension discovers us.'

'Copy that.' Barney popped the last nub of chocolate into his mouth and scrunched up the wrapper. 'I think I may have found it.'

'What makes you think that?' Archie queried, continuing his detailed study of the controls.

'Because it's a shiny new lever . . . And it's labelled *Bridge Control*.'

Archie turned and stared at Barney, who was grinning at him – a line of chocolate around his lips – then ran over to examine the lever.

It was a six-inch column with a black plastic knob on the end. The shaft protruded from a slot in the panel shaped like a capital E. The lever was positioned in the topmost horizontal gate which was labelled with the letter 'U'. The middle gate was labelled 'D' and the bottom one bore the letters 'FF', written in red.

'This must be it,' Archie said excitedly, grabbing the knob. He didn't know what 'FF' stood for but he was pretty sure the top two positions moved the bridge Up and Down.

247

'STOP!' Gemma yelled.

Shocked by Agent X-ray's outburst, he released the lever and spun round.

'What's up?' he demanded.

'Don't look at me,' Gemma replied. 'I didn't say anything.'

'Who did then?'

The agents stood in silent confusion for a moment, then the sound of footsteps from the other side of the room drew their attention.

Archie watched in fear as a grisly man stepped from the gloom. He was about six feet tall with dark skin and a shadow of bristles over his shaved head and square jaw. His face was bisected by one thick black eyebrow, sitting above tiny eyes that were sunken deep into their sockets. As he grinned menacingly he revealed a mouth full of metal. He was wearing a grubby white vest stretched over his powerful torso, and green overalls tied at his waist.

One of his thick muscular arms was wrapped around a young girl's neck – her black hair falling forward as she struggled, hiding her face.

'Touch that lever again and I'll break her neck,' the man promised threateningly in an accent Archie placed

248

somewhere in northern Germany.

'Why would I care what you do to her?' Archie replied, trying to sound as tough as he could. 'Who is she anyway?'

'See for yourself,' the man sneered, gripping the girl's head and yanking it back.

As her hair fell from her face Archie's mouth dropped open in utter confusion. He recognised her crooked fringe and the defiant curl of her mouth but for a moment he couldn't understand what he was seeing.

'Gemma?' he whispered. 'Is that you?'

Chapter 30

Archie's eyes flicked from one Gemma to the other. The one standing at the edge of the fizzing moat looked exactly like his friend and fellow STINKBOMB agent, right down to the tiny details of her tight ponytail and expression of utter contempt. But maybe she was too composed, too perfect?

The other Gemma, struggling in the grip of Evelyn Tension's henchman, wore an unfamiliar expression – one of pure fear. He'd never seen Gemma's hair tangled and loose but she could easily have lost her hair bobble in the struggle with the bad guy – and Archie was in no doubt that the real Gemma would have put up one heck of a struggle.

'One of them must be Evelyn Tension in disguise,'

he muttered through the corner of his mouth. 'But which one?'

Barney shook his head. 'They look identical to me.'

'So how do I tell them apart?'

'Come on, Yankee,' the Gemma by the moat urged, planting her hands on her hips. 'She's a fake – just lower the bridge and let's get on with this.'

'She's right,' the other Gemma offered, her defiant tones grabbing Archie's attention. 'Don't worry about me. You just need to do whatever it takes to rescue Winchester.'

Archie's gaze bounced from one to the other with quickening frequency as he tried desperately to identify the real Agent X-ray. If the Gemma he'd hidden with by the steel cylinder was a fake, then why hadn't she grabbed him there and then? Unless she couldn't be sure of capturing him and Barney at the same time? Then again, if the Gemma being held captive was a fake, would she really encourage him to lower the bridge and call her own bluff? Unless that in itself was a double bluff and the bridge was booby-trapped somehow? He could taste salt on his tongue as sweat trickled over his lip. His mind continued its tightening spirals, guessing and second-guessing the true identities of the two Gemmas in front of him.

'This is ridiculous,' announced the Gemma standing by the moat. 'If you're not going to lower the bridge I will.'

'Hold it right there,' Archie ordered before she had taken her second stride towards him. 'If you take one more step I'll throw you in that acid myself.'

Gemma froze, her eyes narrowed. 'Is that a threat?'

Archie shook his head. 'It's a promise.'

Gemma kept her eyes locked on Archie's for a few seconds and he wondered if she was going to test his resolve, but eventually she relaxed and signalled her compliance with a nod.

If she is really Evelyn Tension, surely she'd have fancied her chances of beating me, one on one? *Archie thought.* Unless Tension had concluded that, having dispatched her guards, he was a force to be reckoned with? Or maybe she just couldn't resist playing one last Evil Genius mind game before she destroyed the world?

The more he tried to figure out the conundrum, the more confused he felt about who was who.

'What do you want from me?' he demanded of the henchman.

'I want you and your tubby friend to lie face down on the floor with your hands behind your heads.'

Archie's eyes flickered towards the circular stage where the lethal laser beam was edging slowly but surely towards Adam Winchester's groin. Even if he could disable the ray-gun he would still have to cross the moat to rescue Adam Winchester.

Archie thought about his options and he knew exactly what was the right thing to do. All his training, the whole philosophy of STINKBOMB's mission to preserve national security, left him in no doubt as to how he ought to proceed.

His training told him to ignore Gemma's safety and pursue his mission's objective, which was to rescue the Prime Minister. To do so he had to lower the bridge.

He could hear Highwater's words in his mind. *One day, as a STINKBOMB agent, you may be called upon to sacrifice someone close to you in order to protect national security.*

One agent's life was a small price to pay for a chance of averting all-out nuclear war. Sacrifice one life to save millions. If it was his own neck on the line he would do it, no question.

But he couldn't bring himself to lower the bridge

and sign Gemma's death warrant. There had to be another way.

'I can't tell them apart,' he said to Barney through the side of his mouth.

'We have to think,' Barney urged. 'Explore every inch of our knowledge.'

'*Knowledge* – that's it!' Archie exclaimed, seeing a chance of distinguishing between the two girls. Addressing both Gemmas, he announced, 'Girls go to college, to get more knowledge.'

'Boys go to Jupiter,' they responded in unison, 'to get more stupider.'

Archie grimaced with frustration. How did the fake Gemma know their codes?

'Girls ace school,' Barney said casually, 'because they're smart and cool.'

Again both Gemmas replied together: 'Boys are smelly and they watch too much telly.'

Archie sighed with exasperation. 'She knows all our passwords,' he muttered, glancing at the lever on the wall. Suddenly it reminded him of an aircraft's landing-gear lever, normally used to lower the undercarriage using hydraulic pressure. But if the hydraulic system is damaged the wheels can still be extended by allowing

254

the gear to free-fall into position. 'FF' – free-fall!

Barney cupped a hand over his mouth. 'She must have access to our mission files. That means she's up to speed with every trick in our book.'

Suddenly a plan flashed into Archie's mind. It was risky, but if it worked they might still have a chance of rescuing the Prime Minister without sacrificing Gemma.

To Barney he muttered, 'In that case we'll just have to test her on something that isn't written in our files. I need you to block their view of this lever.'

Barney shuffled to his left and puffed out his chest.

Turning to the other three people in the Command Room, Archie laughed maniacally. 'I'm having so much fun right now,' he exclaimed. Tightening his grip on the black knob, he slid the lever across and slammed it down, forcing it straight past the 'D' gate and snapping it into the detent marked 'FF'. 'In fact I'd go as far as to say, *I'm having a blast.*'

Pivoting on the ceiling-mounted hinge, the thick metal strut was already halfway through its swing by the time Archie had finished delivering the code. With immense power the huge pendulum accelerated down, gaining rapid momentum as the weight of the gangplank plummeted through a perfect arc. The silence of its progress only seemed to emphasise the lethal power it contained.

Archie caught his breath as the sheer might of what he had unleashed became clear. If the real Gemma failed to react to his coded instruction she would be annihilated, like a condemned building at the mercy of a wrecking ball.

Archie felt a slight breeze on his face as the pendulum forced the air from its path. Suddenly the Gemma who was standing near the moat threw herself to the floor. It seemed to Archie like an age since he'd spoken the code but in reality it was probably a fraction of a second – just long enough for his words to reach her ears, and the electric impulses from her brain to fire her muscles into action.

As the real Gemma hit the deck, pressing herself flat against its cold hard surface, the pendulum reached the bottom of its arc, bridging the toxic moat for just an instant. But its momentum carried it through the vertical position and the section of walkway whistled over Gemma's head, missing her by millimetres.

Continuing its upward swing, the arm of the pendulum possessed considerable force when it struck the fake Gemma and the goon posing as her captor.

Oblivious to the hammer-blow he was about to endure, he took the full force of the impact on his forehead. Grunting loudly as the steel walkway thumped into him, he flew off his feet and crashed across the room before slamming into a control panel.

The replica Gemma seemed to catch a glimpse of the tethered missile as it neared her face and she managed to raise an arm in self-defence. Nevertheless she took a crashing blow to her jaw that sent her sprawling across the floor, coming to rest in a tangled, motionless heap.

The real Gemma raised her head tentatively but quickly ducked again as the massive pendulum whistled millimetres above her again as it swung back towards its original position. When it had passed she scrambled out of its path before it returned on its next swing.

'Well, she got what she deserved,' she said, hauling herself to her feet.

Archie smiled. 'She certainly took it on the chin.'

'I thought she really got into the swing of it,' Barney added, puffing hard as he climbed to his feet.

'You hit the deck too?' Gemma noted. 'I'm impressed, Zulu. I wasn't sure if you'd remember our private little signal.'

Barney's face froze into a smile and he nodded rigidly. When Gemma looked away he cupped a hand to his mouth and whispered to Archie, 'What signal is she talking about?'

'The signal *you* devised,' Archie whispered. *'I'm having a blast* was the code for all agents to drop to the floor. Hang on, what were you doing on the floor then?'

Barney shifted awkwardly. 'I think I may have experienced a momentary suspension of consciousness when the metal ramp connected with that dude's forehead.'

Archie replayed Barney's words in his head for a moment, then his mouth fought to suppress a smile. 'You mean you *fainted*?'

Barney bobbed his head sheepishly. 'I can't really handle the sight of blood.'

A desperate stifled groan from the direction of the round platform reminded Archie that their mission was far from accomplished. Evelyn Tension may well have been neutralised but the fiendish chain reaction of events she had set in motion was still drawing the world towards certain destruction.

The laser beam continued to edge ever closer to the Prime Minister, who was writhing helplessly

258

on the circular slab.

'Come on, let's get him free – quickly!' Archie ordered.

The periodic screech of the ramp dragging on the ground at the bottom of each swing had now ceased. The section of walkway had come to rest balanced between the floor and the rim of the round platform, angled precariously over the boiling moat.

Gemma reached the bridge first, testing its solidity with one foot. Satisfied it would hold firm, she stepped on to the gangway and, holding her arms out for balance, climbed the slope to the platform. As she knelt at Adam Winchester's hand, examining the steel manacle clamped around his wrist, Barney stepped nervously on to the bridge.

Archie stood at the foot of the steel gangplank and as he watched his friend edge gingerly towards the safety of the island, he felt the warm waters of triumph lapping at his toes. All they had to do was get the Prime Minister back to London, discredit his impersonator and put an end to this crisis. No one could stand in their way now.

Then a murderous scream echoed round the Command Room, plunging Archie into an icy sea of absolute terror.

Chapter 31

Archie spun round to see Gemma's double standing upright and looking at her reflection in a glass radar screen. Her lower jaw was twisted to one side, jutting out unnaturally beneath her ear.

'MY FACE!!' she shrieked, looking wildly at Archie. 'Look what you've done to my face. It's ruined!'

'Strictly speaking, that isn't your face at all,' Archie's voice quavered, as he jabbed a thumb over his shoulder. 'It's hers.'

'You'll pay for this, you little oik,' the fake Gemma snarled, slurring slightly due to her jaw being horribly wonky.

She was holding a metal box housing a red and a green button. With a triumphant smirk she punched the red one with the heel of her hand and tossed the box away. Archie heard a mechanical whirr behind him but before he realised what it meant the giant pendulum had started to rotate and the metal gangplank motored into the air, stranding Gemma and Barney on the island.

'Rats,' Barney whispered, clenching his fists. 'I should have known there'd be a portable override remote. There's *always* a portable override remote.'

'Don't worry,' Archie called out. 'We'll cross that bridge when we come to it.'

The fake Gemma dug the nails of her right hand into her own neck just below her left ear, hooking her fingers round a flap of skin. Drawing her hand upward and back across her face, she let out a maniacal scream as she stripped away her disguise.

The mask stretched and peeled off in one rubbery, sticky movement, finally releasing its grip on the impostor's face with an elastic *snap*. The face beneath the mask was pale and slender with piercing green eyes.

'Evelyn Tension,' Archie muttered.

'What a relief,' the woman sighed. 'Those masks are so bad for one's skin, you know.'

The mask hung limply from her hand like a ghoulish head that had been wrenched from its body and had its eyes removed. Evelyn Tension pulled off her wig to reveal a long mane of vivid copper-coloured hair. Then, grimacing and grunting, she grabbed her crooked jaw and yanked, twisting it with a grinding screech back round to its proper position.

She exercised her mouth a couple of times then smiled sweetly at Archie, who couldn't help thinking, in spite of himself, how pretty she now was.

'That's better,' Tension purred, batting her thick dark eyelashes and letting out a girlish giggle. 'Well, well. You must be Archie. Sweet, young Archie.'

Archie couldn't believe what he had just witnessed. The freakish removal of the incredibly lifelike mask, followed by the inhuman way she had relocated her own jaw, told him Evelyn Tension was someone to treat with maximum caution. And yet now she seemed so innocent and kind, making it hard to believe she was capable of being a deadly assassin.

'Now, now, young man,' she scolded playfully, winking slowly. 'Are you planning to take the Prime Minister away from me, you naughty boy?'

Archie cleared his throat. 'I'm afraid so,' he replied. 'The game is up.'

'How do you intend getting back to London

with him?' she asked gently.

Archie found the pleasantries both incongruous and oddly charming, but he also knew Tension was just biding her time. 'Er . . . do you really expect me to stand here and chat all night?'

'Not really, Master Hunt.' She gave a sinister smile. 'I expect you to die!'

As she spoke Evelyn Tension broke into a run, charging at Archie with fury in her eyes.

Standing his ground, Archie waited until his attacker was within range, then ducked low and drove his right fist straight out towards her stomach. It was a textbook punch, timed to perfection and packed full of power.

But it was matched by Tension's blocking manoeuvre, swiping a hand downward and smacking Archie's wrist, sending his punch flying harmlessly wide.

'Aahh!' he yelled, feeling as though his arm had been beaten with an iron bar.

Tension followed up her block by driving the heel of her hand towards the bridge of Archie's nose. The blow could have killed him if it had connected but he saw it coming at the last second and dropped his chin to his chest. Nevertheless the punch caught him square on the forehead and sent him sprawling on to his back, his head overhanging the edge of the bubbling chemical moat. Momentum carried his arms above his head and the knuckles of one hand skimmed the surface of the fluorescent fluid.

Archie's hand recoiled instinctively as the acid scorched his flesh. Glancing at his hand he saw the skin on two knuckles was charred and black – a glimpse of white bone showing on each joint. Grinding his teeth, he growled in agony and rolled away from the edge but, before he could jump to his feet, Evelyn Tension was upon him. Her thighs straddled him and squeezed his ribs tightly.

Archie again saw her punch coming and snapped his head to one side, dodging her fist as it flashed past his ear and plunged into the liquid behind him.

Expecting the acid to strip the flesh from her bones, he waited for the agonised scream that would signal his moment to counterattack. But Evelyn Tension didn't withdraw a skeletal stump from the moat. She didn't even scream. Instead she smiled serenely at Archie, swishing her hand in the acid as if enjoying the refreshing waters of a mountain stream on a summer's day.

'I do so love the feel of Boro-chloro-hydro-sulphur-nucleic acid, don't you?' she enquired, the sweetness in her voice contrasting with the aggressive way she was pushing Archie's head towards the fluid. 'It's so good for one's joints.'

'It's just one of those things I've never got round to trying,' Archie replied, straining to keep his head above the surface.

When Evelyn Tension withdrew her hand Archie understood her immunity to the acid. The glove she had been wearing had been dissolved by the turquoise liquid fizzing by his ear, but her hand had remained unaffected by the acid's flesh-stripping capabilities . . . because it was mechanical.

Tension flexed her robotic hand a few times, admiring the elegant steel fingers and intricate circuitry around her wrist as the acid evaporated, leaving the limb shiny as new.

Fighting against the human arm that was forcing him down towards the corrosive liquid, Archie flailed a hand blindly at Tension's face. His fingertips brushed against the top of her ear and he gripped on to the fleshy lug for all he was worth, dragging her face towards the acid. When she pulled her head back Archie maintained his grip and felt Tension's ear coming away in his hand.

The sound of tearing flesh was so excruciating Archie almost released his handful of skin but he knew the future of the world depended on him winning this battle.

Tension pulled her head back, and as she twisted her face away from Archie, a piece of flesh about two feet long peeled away from her chin, stretching taut between her throat and Archie's grip. When it finally ripped free of Tension's face it recoiled like an elastic band, pinging into Archie's hand. He retched and immediately flung the skin into the bubbling moat, where it dissolved instantly, while Tension seemed unaware that half her face had peeled off. It was as if she felt no pain.

Momentarily terrified by the thought of what state his enemy's face would be in, Archie caught his breath – expecting a bloody skull to turn back to face him. But when Evelyn Tension looked his way he realised that he had not torn a strip of flesh from her face – just another layer of latex mask.

The whole of the lower half of the evil villain's face, along with one cheekbone and an eye socket, was made of steel. A glass eye stared blankly from its exposed hollow like an emerald green bauble.

Large countersunk screws hinged her bottom jaw to

her skull just in front of where her ears were supposed to be. Her mouth was lined with perfect white dentures, but without the frame of her plump lips her smile was like the crazy grin of a ventriloquist's dummy.

'Now, now,' she teased, apparently unaware that she had lost half her face. 'Play nice, Archie, or you won't have any friends.'

'I will if you will,' Archie replied with a grimace.

'Leave him alone,' Gemma yelled from the platform.

Barney stood with his toes overhanging the edge of the moat, as if considering leaping across. Apparently thinking better of it, he growled, 'Man, I wish I could get across there and kick your butt.'

'If I were you, heaven forbid, I'd be very careful what I wished for, young man.' Letting out an evil laugh, Tension shoved Archie's head further back towards the acid. He could feel the vile concoction spitting on to his hair, singeing his scalp. If he didn't do something pretty soon, the top of his skull was going to be submerged and the fight would be over.

Suddenly remembering the magno-pen he had hidden in the leg of his wetsuit, Archie reached down to his ankle and slipped it out. Articulating the fingers of one hand he twisted its barrel to arm the device but before he could click the button on its end, Tension snatched it from his grip.

'Naughty, naughty,' she scolded, tossing the gadget across the room. 'I know they say the pen is mightier than the sword –' her playful expression hardened instantly into one of murderous intent – 'but the bionic arm is mightier than the lot.'

With that her mechanical hand flashed down, gripping Archie's shoulder with such force that searing nerve-shredding pain shot through every extremity of his body.

He tried to fight her off, willing his fists to fly at her freakish half-human face – but his arms just lay limply at his sides. If he could just raise a knee he might be able to lever her over his head and into the chemical pool. But his legs didn't respond with even so much as a twitch.

'Poor Archie,' Tension soothed. 'It seems as though I've touched a nerve. I can tell you're trying so hard to fight me off but your body just won't play ball, will it?'

Archie wanted to scream in agony and yell out in protest at the white-hot pain inside him, but he couldn't even open his mouth. The only part of his body he was able to move were his eyeballs, which was ironic because they were about the only part of his body he didn't want to move. He wanted to keep them locked on his enemy.

'So it appears I have the upper hand?' Evelyn Tension arched one eyebrow but her subtle expression of cool superiority was spoiled by her metal mouth being clenched into a permanently manic grin.

'What are you doing to him?' Gemma shouted angrily from the island. 'Leave him alone.'

'This is what I call the *Over Grip*,' Tension announced, her voice oozing with self-satisfaction. 'Because when I use it, it's all over. Actually maybe I should call it the *All Over Grip*? Or how about something slightly more devilish like – oh, what about the *Numbifier*? You know, like Mummifier but *Numbi*fier – because it makes your whole body numb. Oooh, that's *divine*.'

Gemma's lip curled into an angry snarl. 'How about calling it the *You'll be sorry when I get my hands on you-ifier*?'

'Bravo!' Tension enthused condescendingly. 'I do admire your pluck, young lady. Unfortunately you won't get your grubby little hands on me because you'll never make it off that platform alive. And poor Archie here can't help you because I have immobilised his entire body by applying an inhuman amount of pressure to his suprascapular nerve endings. His entire body is currently infused with such an enormous amount of pain that his brain is unable to process any motor function impulses . . . When I put it like that, I suppose the Numbifier isn't such a good name after all. Sounds rather peaceful, doesn't it?'

Maintaining her grip on Archie's shoulder, Evelyn Tension climbed off him as if dismounting a horse and stood up, holding him off the ground at arm's length. Archie's body hung completely lifeless from her bionic fist, like a wet towel. His arms sagged by his sides and his head lolled helplessly to one side. He could feel a string of gooey saliva trickling from the corner of his mouth, which was gaping open, and his tongue flopped out like a thirsty dog.

'Let him go right now,' Barney shouted, fury raising the pitch of his voice.

As Evelyn Tension turned to face Barney, she swung Archie round so that he was hanging over the bubbling blue-green acid.

'Whatever you say.'

Chapter 32

Evelyn Tension giggled naughtily. 'But first I want to tell you about my delicious plot to take over the world. And when you have heard what I have to say, you will agree that I am the most despicable, the most devious and the evilest mastermind ever in the history of the world.' Flicking her hair off one shoulder she added, 'As well as being the most beautiful . . . obviously.'

'Talk about *crazy*,' Gemma muttered.

'I know,' Barney mumbled. 'Has she even *looked* in a mirror?'

Evelyn Tension swung Archie away from the acid and walked towards the entrance hatch, dragging him behind her like a sack of rubbish. Propping him up against the periscope, she leaned close to his ear and whispered, 'Just lie here and relax, there's a good boy. You'll be able to speak in a minute or so but it'll take much longer for you to get movement back in your limbs. I just want you to hear all about how fabulous I am.' She stroked his hair with maternal affection. 'Then I'm going to kill you.'

All sorts of defiant words went through Archie's mind but he couldn't get his mouth to move, so he drooled instead.

'Here comes the Evil Mastermind monologue,' Barney muttered to Gemma. 'I reckon we've got about five minutes until crunch time.'

Tension spun round and strutted a few paces towards the edge of the moat, where she stopped, hands on hips. Then she turned, with a lingering look over her shoulder, and sashayed back towards Archie.

'I, Evelyn Tension, have succeeded in my plan to plant a fake Prime Minister in Ten Downing Street.' Pausing to glare down at Archie, she spun round and strutted back the other way. 'In less than four hours the world will see Britain's beloved Prime Minister, Adam Winchester, launch a nuclear attack on Switzerland that will plunge the world into a self-destructive apocalyptical Armageddon.' Pausing for dramatic effect, she dropped her chin and held Gemma's gaze, then shrieked. 'The world will be totally destroyed!'

'Yeah,' Gemma sneered. 'I worked that out from the *self-destructive apocalyptical Armageddon* bit.'

'But here comes the real genius of my plan,' Tension purred, turning and striding towards Archie. 'Here comes the part that is so beautiful, it's almost as perfect as I am.'

'Is it that you'll survive the nuclear fallout because you're going to stay underwater?' Archie slurred.

'I will survive the nuclear fallout,' Tension announced grandly, 'because I'm going to stay down here underwater – wait, you just said that!'

Archie tried to shrug but his shoulders didn't move – although he thought he felt one of his muscles twitch.

'No, no, here's the beautiful part,' Tension asserted, wagging her steel finger at Archie. 'The beautiful part is that the real Adam Winchester will get to watch himself start World War Three just before that laser beam reaches him. It is powerful enough to cut through steel like a knife through butter. Just imagine what it will do to our poor Mr Winchester. He will end his life knowing that the world holds him responsible for its ultimate demise.'

Archie glanced past the crazy assassin's shoulder and noticed a TV screen suspended high above the round platform. It faced directly downward, transmitting 24-hour rolling news coverage of the impending nuclear crisis to its captive audience.

'Isn't it a bit dangerous having a laser capable of cutting through steel on a submarine constructed of, you know, steel?' Archie mumbled, feeling his lips tingling.

'The slab Mr Winchester is tied to is three metres thick and made of steel reinforced with layers of fibreglass mesh. The laser's programmed to reach the PM's delicate flesh at five minutes past midnight. Just after he's seen himself end the world. Provided the laser doesn't stray off course, no harm will come to the rest of the ship.'

'What's he ever done to you?' Gemma called.

'What's he ever done to me?' Tension snarled. 'Oh, nothing much. Apart from making me forsake my whole family in order to do his government's dirty work, then tear up my licence to kill and authorise another British agent to rub me out.'

Archie felt his fingers tingling and he moved his chin an inch to the left. 'You missed out the part where you

274

started working as a hired assassin, taking contracts from foreign criminals. You even targeted members of the British Foreign Office.'

'Oh, come on!' Tension complained. 'What difference are a few extra hits going to make to the price of fish?'

'They were innocent people,' Archie exclaimed.

'But the money was *sooo* good,' said Tension sulkily. 'I mean, how's a girl supposed to stock her designer wardrobe on a government salary alone? And the jobs were a doddle too. Money for old rope – usually tied into a noose and slung over a roof beam.' Her brittle laugh echoed round the Command Room's steel panelling.

'And what about working as a double agent?' Barney chipped in. 'Selling secrets to the Russians is cheap. Really cheap.'

'You obviously don't know what I was charging, darling,' Tension quipped.

Watching Evelyn Tension brag and strut like a peacock, Archie detected something tragic about her. Yes, she was insane and psychotic, but there was something vulnerable about her too, almost sad.

'It's not my fault I ended up here anyway,' she said. 'I blame my father.'

'What did he do?' Archie asked gently.

Evelyn Tension stopped and turned to him, looking reflective for a moment.

'When I was ten my father didn't buy me a pony for my birthday,' she said softly.

'I see,' Archie replied. 'So you were disappointed? Maybe you felt he didn't love you?'

'Disappointed? No way,' Evelyn Tension sneered. 'I hated ponies. That's why it was so cool that he bought me a Glock 17 pistol. As soon as I held it in my hands I knew I wanted to shoot people when I grew up.'

'Every little girl has to have a dream,' Archie mumbled.

'I wanted to be a ballerina,' Gemma whispered.

Barney nodded absently.

Archie's eyes flicked to a small object less than a metre from his right hand. With a huge effort he walked his fingers a couple of inches towards it, freezing when his captor looked his way.

'I gave up everything for this country,' Tension shrieked, her normal eye bulging almost as wide as her mechanical eyeball. 'I lost my friends, my family, my identity, just so I could sneak around the world doing the government's dirty work. Adam Winchester's dirty work.'

'You volunteered to be trained as a Scalpel,' Archie pointed out. 'And according to your records you didn't have many friends.'

Tension stalked towards Archie and towered over him, squeezing her fists tightly. 'You are an impudent little boy,' she breathed angrily. 'I shall take great pleasure in killing you.'

Archie rolled his eyes to look at his tormentor. 'You swore to protect our country,' he said. 'But you turned out to be just another common criminal.'

'My dear boy,' Tension giggled and sighed. 'I can assure you there's nothing common about me.'

A laboured groan drew everyone's attention across the room. To Archie's utter amazement, Evelyn Tension's goon was slowly climbing to his feet.

The man had taken the full force of the swinging steel gangplank right between his eyes but was now fully conscious. It was like seeing someone come back from the dead. As he drew himself to his full height Archie understood how he had survived the immense blow he'd sustained.

He had a wide gash in his forehead that was trickling blood down his craggy face. The wound gaped open, revealing a wide expanse of his skull, but it was not

277

made of clean white bone – it was made of steel.

'Oh, brother,' Archie muttered. 'Now we've got two bionic villains to deal with.'

'My darling, you're awake,' said Evelyn Tension softly. 'How's your poor head?'

The man's dark eyebrow lowered and he growled, showing two rows of teeth clad in shining metal. 'You,' he barked, pointing at Archie. 'Look what you did to my head. I'm going to kill you for this.'

'I saw him first, Klaus,' Tension said. 'Young Archie here is my handsome prize, and I'm going to savour wringing his perfect little neck. I'm afraid you'll just have to make do with the other two.'

'We're not some sort of shoddy consolation prize you know,' Gemma shouted. Shaking her head at Barney she muttered, 'The cheek of it.'

'Did you say *Klaus*?' Archie enquired. 'Not Klaus Von Grosskopf – the world-renowned robotics and explosives professor?'

'The one and only,' the man replied, expanding his muscular chest.

Archie resisted the urge to frown, maintaining the pretence that he still had no control of his slack features. 'I thought you assassinated him? There's a whole MI6

278

file about Professor Von Grosskopf's plot to blow up Buckingham Palace by packing a robotic corgi with C-5 explosives.'

'I was *sent* on a mission to kill him,' Tension confirmed. 'As I recall, we had quite a ding-dong, didn't we, Klausy?'

'We did, Evie,' Klaus chuckled. 'You cracked my skull with a monkey wrench, then I scorched your hand with a blowtorch . . .'

Evelyn Tension sniggered like a love-struck schoolgirl. 'Do you remember how you broke my jaw with a headbutt just as I was about to slip the cheese wire around your neck?'

'Sounds romantic,' Archie mumbled, walking his hand a few centimetres closer to the slender silver object by his side. 'I suppose you'd call it love at first fight.'

'In the end we both realised we'd met our match,' Tension announced, sliding two metal fingers into the brute's monstrous hand. 'After Klaus had patched us both up with a few additional features here and there – a new arm for me, steel plates over the skull for himself – we decided to think of a way we could make our mark on the world. One night I mentioned something about MI6's shelved Gemini Project and

279

immediately his piggy little eyes lit up. He was sure he would be able to iron out any problems with its design if I could get him the prototype Face-mapping-quick-drying-liquid-latex-mask-gun.'

'So you stole the gun?' Gemma said accusingly.

'Oh please, don't get so high and mighty with me, young lady.' As Tension turned to address Gemma, Archie slid his hand along the floor another few centimetres. 'MI6 had finished with the project. They couldn't get it to work so they gave up on it. It was my Klausy's genius that brought the idea to life.'

'Is it just me or does anyone else want to puke when she calls him that?' Gemma muttered.

'So which of you is the real brains behind this scheme?' Archie asked, stalling for time.

'We're a team, aren't we, Klausy?' Tension answered shrilly. 'We both contribute equally. It's fifty-fifty.'

The professor nodded his shaved head with satisfaction. Unable to contain herself, Tension continued. 'I mean, I probably had the original idea to kidnap the PM and use the mask-gun to plant an impostor in his place and it was definitely my brainwave to instigate a nuclear war. Come to think of it, stealing this decommissioned submarine from a naval scrapyard was certainly my idea – as was bribing a crew of submariners to desert from the Chinese navy. When it came to selecting someone to fill in for the PM, I immediately thought of asking Klaus's brother, who is exactly the right build, and I trained him to mimic Adam Winchester's mannerisms exactly. Gosh, listen to me! It sounds like I'm saying all this is down to me . . . and I suppose most of it is, but Klaus definitely played his part. A small but very crucial part.'

'I did discover that rubber with a bond-length of eighty picometres was the perfect consistency for the mask-gun,' Klaus insisted sulkily.

Tension patted Klaus's hand. 'Like I said, Klausy, you played a *small* part.'

Klaus ground his teeth and stifled a small growl. Archie deduced that Von Grosskopf was probably well used to biting his tongue and suppressing his feelings around Tension.

Archie edged his hand across the floor a few more centimetres. The feeling was returning to his legs, tingling up his shins, and he would soon have to make his move.

'So your brother is posing as the PM?' said Archie, still trying to give himself longer to recover.

281

'It's his twin brother Kurt,' Tension explained. 'They're not identical though. Kurt is much shorter and he doesn't have Klausy's good looks.'

Archie glanced at the professor's Neanderthal features and grimaced. 'Poor old Kurt,' he muttered.

'I've got his nose,' Klaus announced eagerly.

'That's nice.'

'And his ears and one of his eyes,' Klaus added. 'I keep them in a jar by my bed.'

'Klaus cut them off with a penknife when they were kids,' Tension added quickly – as though this extra information cast Klaus's souvenirs in a better light. 'He and his brother were playing doctors – or craniofacial plastic surgeons, to be precise. Boys will be boys!'

'I keep my brother's features next to my bed to remind me of the fun we used to have together.'

'He's very attached to them,' said Tension.

Archie snorted. 'Unlike his brother.'

'Now I'm tired of talking,' Tension barked angrily. 'It's time to get rid of these nuisances so we can concentrate on destroying the world. Klaus, be a sweetie would you, and kill them.'

'Wait!' Archie protested, desperate for a few more seconds of recuperation. Klaus paused expectantly.

282

Archie racked his brains for a reason to have interrupted the proceedings but his mind was blank. 'You'll never get away with this!'

Not exactly original, Archie thought. But better than nothing.

'But we already have, my love,' Tension bragged.

Archie knew his time was up. With a gargantuan effort he slid his hand across the floor and grabbed the object he'd had his eye on – the magno-pen Tension had tossed away earlier – and cupped his hand over it. All he had to do was distract the two villains long enough to arm the pen and charge it up for ten seconds. Then he would let them have it.

'How long do you think you can survive underwater?' Archie asked, trying to twist the pen's barrel with his thumb.

'As long as it takes,' Tension whispered. 'When the nuclear radiation clears we will surface and reveal the despicable trick we have played on the world. We will be known far and wide as the two most odious and attractive criminal masterminds the world has ever known.'

'Attractive?' Archie sneered. 'With that metal mouth?'

283

'Come, come, Archie, don't be cruel,' Tension coaxed. 'Klaus's braces are just a temporary measure to correct a rather pronounced overbite.'

'Er . . . I wasn't talking about Klaus!' Archie laughed. 'It's you who looks like the bride of Frankenstein.'

Urgently Tension strode to the nearest glass screen and peered curiously at her reflection. Slowly her steel jaw fell open and her hand went up to her cheek.

'My face,' she gasped in disbelief, patting her chin as if to confirm what her eyes were telling her. Then her embarrassment curdled into fury and spewed out in an ear-splitting wail directed at Von Grosskopf. 'MY BEAUTIFUL FACE! Why didn't you tell me? You know I never appear in public without my face on! I've never been so humiliated in all my life!'

As Evelyn Tension railed at the dumbfounded professor, Archie managed to twist the magno-pen's barrel. With all the concentration he could muster he willed his muscles to lift his arm, jabbing the pen against his thigh to extend the ballpoint, and aimed it at the two villains.

As soon as the pen had charged up he would let them have it.

'Ten . . .' he whispered to himself. 'Nine . . . eight . . .'

284

Chapter 33

'Seven . . . six . . . five . . .'

Evelyn Tension shrieked furiously at Klaus. 'How would you like it if I let you strut around with food on your face, or your flies open?'

Von Grosskopf shrugged his mighty shoulders like a sullen teenager. 'I wouldn't be bothered.'

'Four . . . three . . .'

'*I wouldn't be bothered*,' Tension mimicked. 'Well, we'll see about that. Just you wait!'

Archie could feel his pulse racing, his palms sweating. 'Two . . . one . . .'

'Why are you shouting at me anyway?' complained the professor. 'The kid must have been the one who pulled your mask off.'

Evelyn Tension turned to look at Archie with an expression of dawning realisation – as if she had completely forgotten that he was in the room.

'Zero,' Archie whispered. 'Now I just point and shoot.'

'YOU!' Tension hissed, her normal eye narrowing accusingly. 'You'll pay for this. Nobody humiliates Evelyn Tension and lives to tell the tale.'

'Is that so?' Archie replied casually, tilting the pen so that it was aimed directly at the two villains. 'I'm afraid you might be in for a bit of a shock.' With a small movement of his thumb he fired the magno-pen.

Archie waited for the electromagnetic pulse to flatten his enemies – but nothing happened.

He clicked the pen again, but still nothing.

'I was going to kill you anyway,' Tension bragged. 'But now I'm going to take extra pleasure in watching you suffer.'

As the crazed assassin stalked closer to Archie he felt his hopes wither. He should have known better than to rely on one of Holden Grey's gadgets, he thought ruefully. Looking dejectedly at the pen in his hand, he clicked it one more time.

Again the pen didn't unleash its immobilising electric

286

charge, but Archie finally understood precisely why.

His thumb hadn't moved.

Obviously his nerve endings were still confused by Tension's death grip. Somehow the signal from his brain to his hand must have been diverted or scrambled or something. And even though his brain had received a return signal telling it that its command had been carried out, Archie's thumb was as limp as a raw sausage.

Which meant that maybe, just maybe, the magno-pen wasn't useless after all. Archie felt a surge of hope . . . then Evelyn Tension bent over him and plucked the pen from his hand.

'Well, well, well,' Tension marvelled, examining the slender case pinched between her thumb and forefinger. 'What do we have here? If I'm not very much mistaken, it's an MI6 magno-pen.' She twisted the pen's barrel, disarming the device. 'How very quaint! Not only does the Secret Service send a bunch of children to stop me destroying the world but they send you armed with a gadget straight out of 1967.' Tension giggled with amusement, flipping the pen in her hand as she crossed the Command Room towards the acid moat. 'I didn't realise what this was when I took it from you earlier,' she said, turning to face Archie again.

287

'Be careful,' he warned. 'It's not a toy.'

'Oh, be quiet!' Tension shrieked, jabbing the pen in Archie's direction. 'I was a secret agent for twenty years. I was using gadgets in the field before you were even born.'

Slumped against the periscope, Archie wondered if he could use Evelyn Tension's fiery indignation against her. 'That *was* a long time ago,' he said patronisingly. 'You haven't been an active field agent for *years*. It's amazing how quickly you forget your training when you're out of practice.'

'I can promise you I've never been sharper.'

'Maybe so,' Archie replied reasonably. 'But I would still prefer you not to mess around with the magno-pen. I wouldn't want you to hurt yourself.'

'Oh please! The magno-pen was the simplest weapon in the MI6 arsenal.' Tension threw her thick red hair back and cackled. 'Twist-click-click – simple! When this thing knocks you out I'll get Klaus here to dunk you in the acid. All that'll be left of you will be your oversized feet.' She twisted the barrel angrily and pointed the pen at Archie.

'I wouldn't do that if I were you,' Archie advised. 'Honestly, I really wouldn't . . .'

'Nice knowing you, Archie,' Tension sneered triumphantly.

288

CLICK. CLICK.

The sharp explosive snap was accompanied by a brilliant white flash. Evelyn Tension stood motionless, eyes and mouth wide open. Her smooth glossy hair was now scorched and frizzy, shooting out from her head in all directions as if she was in freefall. Grey smoke curled from the barrel of the pen and the top of her head, while worms of blue light crackled from her fingertips like lightning. For a split second she teetered on the spot, still frozen with the backfiring pen aimed at Archie.

Then, like a falling tree, she toppled backwards, pivoting on her heels as she plunged into the bubbling turquoise pool behind her with a resounding SPLOSH.

Klaus Von Grosskopf emitted an anguished groan as he watched the acid moat swallow his partner in crime. After a few moments a single glass eyeball bobbed eagerly to the surface, confirming her fate.

'What have you done?' Von Grosskopf snarled at Archie, his dark eyebrow dipping sharply at its centre.

'I tried to warn her,' he said innocently. 'But she wouldn't listen.'

'She shot herself,' Gemma said. 'At point-blank range.'

'Ballpoint-blank range, to be precise,' Archie added.

289

Barney stood at the edge of the round platform and peered into the moat. 'Well, nobody could say she didn't throw herself into her work.'

'I'm sorry, Klaus,' Archie called. 'But I think your partnership has been dissolved. Or at least your partner has.'

Snorting and snarling, Klaus Von Grosskopf charged towards Archie, who still didn't have full control of his limbs. The hulking scientist grabbed Archie roughly by one shoulder and hauled him off the ground, examining him at arm's length.

'Call me impatient,' Klaus leered. 'But I can't wait until midnight to see Winchester sliced in half.' With his free hand he rummaged in his overalls, produced a small key fob and pressed the button on it. Immediately the laser's progress towards the Prime Minister accelerated visibly. Smirking evilly, Klaus continued: 'Now I'd say you've got about five minutes to save him – so tell me, kid, what's the next part of your brilliant plan?'

'I'm glad you asked me that,' Archie answered with a confident chuckle.

But his insides were churning and his half-numb limbs were trembling because the truth was, he didn't have a plan.

Chapter 34

With a tremendous scream pitched somewhere between triumph and rage, Klaus Von Grosskopf hurled Archie across the Command Room, sending him sprawling into a bank of control panels.

Archie took the force of the impact on one shoulder, coming to rest slumped over on his knees.

Man, that's going to hurt when I get my full feeling back, he thought.

Archie tried to lever himself to a standing position, but his legs still felt like they belonged to someone else. Before he was even halfway upright he felt Klaus grab two fistfuls of the back of his wetsuit and hoist him off the floor.

'Put him down, you metal-mouthed, mono-browed mega-freak,' Gemma yelled.

'Nobody tells me what to do,' Klaus roared. 'Not any more.'

Suspended belly down, Archie felt Klaus rocking him gently back and forth.

Recognising the little practice swings that precede a launch, a new plan began to form in Archie's mind. 'I *forbid* you from throwing me at the wall just to the right of the entrance hatch,' he commanded.

'Oh, you *forbid* me, do you?' Klaus sneered. 'Well try this for size.'

With a grunt of effort Klaus launched Archie into the air, aiming him directly at the spot he had been forbidden from targeting.

Archie sailed across the room, limbs hanging down uselessly, and crashed into the wall, this time taking the full force to the side of his body.

'I think I could get used to being the boss around here,' Klaus grinned, brushing his palms together.

Shaking off the pain shooting round his skull, Archie pawed clumsily at the wall. While pretending he was trying to pull himself to his feet, he secretly grabbed the *Bridge Control* lever and slotted it into the gate marked with a D.

Within seconds Klaus was on top of Archie again,

spinning him round and lifting him by the front of his wetsuit. Over his tormentor's shoulder Archie watched the huge pendulum set in motion, swinging the bridge into position over the moat. If Klaus turned round now he would see what Archie had done and immediately return the lever to the 'up' position.

'You'll never be the boss around here,' Archie croaked, stalling for time. 'Now I *absolutely forbid* you from putting me down gently and throwing yourself in the moat.'

'Oh you do, do you?' Klaus chuckled. 'Well, like I said – *nobody* tells me what to do any more.' He lowered Archie gently to the floor but then a frown tugged his single thick eyebrow low over his tiny eyes. 'Hang on a minute!' Klaus lifted Archie's feet clear of the floor again. 'Do you take me for some kind of halfwit?'

'Worth a try,' Archie shrugged sheepishly. 'You geniuses can be really dense sometimes.'

Archie watched the pendulum reach the vertical – and Gemma tiptoe over the gangplank. Barney remained on the platform, trying to prise open the manacles restraining Adam Winchester's wrists.

'There's a laser-guidance panel somewhere,' Archie called.

293

'I know there is,' Klaus replied. 'I built this place. It's over on the far wall. And why are you shouting? I'm right here.'

'I've found the controls,' Gemma yelled. 'What should I do?'

'Remove the panel,' Barney called. 'Cut the wire connecting the battery to the timing display. That should do the trick.'

'There's two wires,' Gemma called. 'A red one and a black one.'

'Cut the red one,' Barney replied emphatically. 'Definitely red . . . No, wait. Black, it's black.'

As Klaus advanced Archie sent a jab straight on to his lantern jaw and the goon staggered back a few paces.

'Is that your final answer?' Gemma insisted. 'Because I don't think we've got time for you to phone a friend.'

'Black,' Barney yelped. 'Cut the black wire.'

'Whatever you say.' Gemma looped the black wire over the serrated blade and sharply drew the knife up, severing the cable. Instantly the laser died.

Archie breathed a sigh of relief. Then the hairs on his neck bristled as he realised Klaus was grinning triumphantly.

294

The laser gun suddenly emitted a series of short sharp buzzes and spluttered back to life. Now it was travelling even faster – making alarmingly quick progress towards the Prime Minister.

Chapter 35

Barney grimaced. 'It must have a back-up power source.' He glanced over his shoulder at the scorching trail advancing between Adam Winchester's legs. 'And I think it was fitted with an anti-tamper booby-trap.'

'At this rate it's not going to take much more than thirty seconds to reach its target,' Archie guessed.

Adam Winchester struggled frantically and tried to shout out, one eye open with wild panic.

Suddenly Klaus lunged at Archie who jumped clumsily backwards, then threw a couple of punches that landed lamely on the professor's muscular chest.

'What do I do?' Gemma yelled.

'Cut the all the wires,' Barney urged. 'One of them might connect to the back-up power source.'

'You're wasting your time,' Klaus called over his shoulder swinging out an arm to grab Archie. Having finally recovered full feeling in his limbs, Archie was suffering the agony of the ordeal his body had been through. The pain would have been unbearable were it not for the adrenalin surging through him and he lurched to one side leaving the professor clawing fresh air.

Archie retaliated with his favourite move. Leaning back with his weight on his right foot he kicked out with his left, driving his heel at his enemy's solar plexus.

But Archie's leg didn't extend with quite its usual snap and Klaus had time to recover his balance and react. Raising his hands to his chest he caught Archie's foot, snatching it mid-flight as if it was a football. Gripping Archie's heel and toes he shoved hard, grinning as the boy hopped frantically backwards to prevent himself toppling over.

'I've cut all the wires,' Gemma announced.

'No good.' Barney glanced ruefully at the intense light beam, now just a few centimetres from the Prime Minister.

Still holding Archie's foot, Klaus was steering him towards the moat.

297

'Zulu, do something!' Gemma shrieked, glancing at the laser.

Smoke started to rise where the beam was scorching the material of Adam Winchester's trousers.

Archie felt the edge of the moat under his heel. He tried to force the professor back but his other foot was too high to afford him any drive.

'X-ray, get over here now,' Barney yelled.

Gemma sprinted back across the bridge.

'Get on all fours,' Barney instructed. 'Trust me.'

Frowning quizzically, Gemma obliged.

Archie knew Klaus had only to push him back another ten centimetres and he would be plunged into the all-consuming acid – and there was nothing he could do about it.

Barney took a couple of steps back. Scrunching his face up with determination, he ran towards Gemma, stepping on to her back and launching himself into the air.

'Su-per-Zulu!' he exclaimed as, with uncharacteristic agility, he leaped across the platform – arms and legs flailing. But as he reached the top of his trajectory it seemed as though he had missed his target. As he started to fall, Barney stretched desperately above his head and his fingertips touched the barrel of the laser gun.

Archie looked into the cold beady eyes of the man who was about to kill him. Suddenly a brilliant white light flashed momentarily across Klaus's face. The intensely bright spot passed quickly from the professor's left ear lobe to his right temple then, almost instantaneously, it was gone.

Remaining completely still, Von Grosskopf stared at Archie with a smug grin fixed on his coarse face.

'Come on then,' Archie goaded, glancing back at the bubbling blue-green acid awaiting him. 'Let's get this over with.'

Klaus didn't move.

Then Archie noticed a wisp of smoke rising from the right side of the goon's eyebrow. A moment later a straight red line appeared across Klaus's brow and a thick crimson liquid started to trickle down his face. Archie suddenly understood what that bright light must have been.

Still grinning, Von Grosskopf released Archie's foot and let his hands drop to his sides. Klaus fell to his knees and the top half of his head, which had been cleanly sliced through by the laser, was jarred loose by the impact. The bloody dome slid down the angled cleft through his skull, toppled on to his shoulder and bounced on to

299

the floor. Archie leaped out of the way as Klaus's lifeless body slumped forward, sprawling over the edge of the moat and sliding into the boiling chemicals.

Relieved and shaken, Archie turned and beamed at Barney who was clambering to his feet on the platform, his cheeks pink with exertion. His intervention had slewed the gun away from the Prime Minister, swinging the laser beam around the Command Room and leaving it pointing at the ceiling.

'Nice work, Agent Zulu,' Archie said. 'Or should I call you Super-Zulu?'

'You can just call me Super,' Barney replied, blushing.

'I can't believe you did that,' Gemma marvelled, getting to her feet.

'I was only risking my life to save a fellow agent.' Barney shrugged. 'It was no biggie.'

'I meant I can't believe you actually managed to *jump*.' Gemma smiled as she jogged over the bridge to study the control panels.

'Listen, thanks,' said Archie. 'I really put my foot in it with Klaus, didn't I?'

'Don't worry about it,' Barney replied. 'I think his invention went to his head in the end.'

'By the way,' Archie said, nodding to the scorched

300

trail veering across the platform and over Adam Winchester's ankle. 'Good thinking – using the manacle to protect the PM's leg. Otherwise he'd have been going back to London in two pieces.'

Barney's cheeks instantly lost their reddish hue. 'All part of the plan,' he laughed unconvincingly.

'Guys, I think I've found the Manacle Release Mechanism,' Gemma called.

She turned a dial, flicked a series of switches and the four metal cuffs sprang open. Barney helped the Prime Minister to his feet and they both edged gingerly over the gangplank.

Adam Winchester gratefully shook hands with each of the agents. Gemma reached up to peel the silver duct tape from over his mouth but he recoiled and shook his head urgently, mumbling unintelligibly and gesturing to his face.

'I think he's saying that Evelyn Tension glued the tape to his face with super-strength adhesive,' Barney reported. 'If you pull it off it will remove half of his face. It's perforated so he can breathe OK but it can only be removed by applying a chemical solvent.'

Adam Winchester nodded rapidly to confirm Barney's translation.

Archie and Gemma exchanged looks of incredulity. 'Dare I ask how you can understand him?' Gemma enquired.

Barney beamed. 'If you'd seen as many spy films as I have, you'd be able to speak fluent Gaglish too.'

'Gaglish?' Archie repeated.

'Uh-huh,' Barney replied, as if perplexed by his friend's ignorance. 'Gaglish is the particular dialect of English spoken by anyone wearing a gag.'

Archie felt a cold wet drop land on his arm. Instinctively he looked up, as if inspecting the sky for rainclouds, and his mood darkened.

The laser beam had burned a hole in the roof of the Command Room about the size of a squash ball. But as well as the ceiling immediately above them Archie knew the laser had scorched its way through the submarine's outer skin – because sea water was now gushing through the hole.

'The laser's breeched the hull!' he said.

'We're looking at Dakota Level flotation capability,' Barney remarked, studying the roof. 'Possibly Level Indianapolis.'

'Which means?' Gemma probed.

Barney pursed his lips gravely. 'We're sinking. Fast.'

Chapter 36

'This way!' Archie yelled. 'Hurry, we don't have much time.'

The water was sloshing over his ankles as he ran towards the doorway. By the time he'd ducked through the hatch and waded along the walkway to the ladder he was waist deep in a fast moving current.

'You go first,' he called to Gemma, at the foot of the ladder. 'Take the Prime Minister to the safety-hatch we came in through.'

'What about you?'

'I'll be right behind you. We need to get the PM out of here.'

Gemma nodded once and scurried up the ladder.

The water was gushing from the command room

like swirling river rapids and Archie had to grip the ladder firmly. Adam Winchester was next up, followed by Barney. As his friend's feet receded above him Archie lifted one foot to the first rung.

Unknown to Archie, the floodwater had dislodged a fire extinguisher from its mounting and was dragging it along the floor. Just as he was about to climb the ladder the heavy steel cylinder struck Archie's standing leg, knocking it from under him. He slipped and fell under the water, which closed around him like an icy fist, squeezing the breath from his lungs.

Floundering beneath the angry torrent Archie struggled to hold on to the ladder but his hands were frozen and his strength was failing. He knew if he lost his grip he'd be swept down into the bowels of the submarine – never to draw breath again. Agonisingly he felt his grip start to loosen and his fists began to unfurl. The rung slipped from his fingers and the force of the water took over him.

Archie knew he was powerless to resist. He closed his eyes and relaxed, surrendering himself to the overwhelming force of the ocean. But suddenly something gripped his outstretched arm, pulling him against the might of the current. His eyes sprang open

304

and he saw a hand clasping his wrist, pulling him back towards the ladder, which he grabbed with renewed determination.

'Thanks,' he said.

Barney nodded. 'You looked a little out of your depth.'

'I was getting a bit carried away.' Archie smiled wryly. 'How did you know to come back for me?'

'When the hero stays behind until last, he always encounters some kind of trouble. *Everyone* knows that.'

Suddenly the submarine lurched, throwing the boys against the railing.

'We're sinking,' Archie said, urging Barney along the walkway, which was now angled steeply downward.

The floodwater had swamped the lower level and was surging up through the metal grille of the walkway. Archie and Barney pelted along the narrow corridor. The torrent echoed louder and louder as the flood gained on them, coursing rapidly through the sub's narrow corridors. Within seconds the water level had risen to their knees.

'Hurry!' Archie yelled, struggling to make himself heard over the metallic roar of the flood.

Frantically they ducked through the hatch in the

bulkhead and sloshed towards the exit. The inner hatch of the airlock was open and Gemma and Adam Winchester were inside the capsule, which was already half full of floodwater. Archie and Barney clambered in and pulled the hatch shut spinning the inner handle to lock it.

Adam Winchester was just zipping up a black wetsuit – flexing his knees as he hauled the fastener up to his chin.

'Where did that come from?' Archie asked.

Gemma shrugged and jabbed her thumb at a recess in the curved wall that was covered by a piece of shattered glass.

Barney read out the label above the compartment. 'Emergency wetsuit: break glass in case of sinking.'

'Handy,' Archie commented. 'And it happens to be a perfect fit too.'

'There were no masks or oxygen cylinders in there though.' Gemma held up the three sets of STINKBOMB scuba gear she'd recovered from their alcove. 'So we're one short.'

'Mr Winchester can have mine,' Archie said, firmly passing a mask and air tank to the Prime Minister. 'I'll hold my breath.'

306

'You'll never make it,' Barney said plaintively. 'Who knows how far we've sunk? It could be minutes before we reach the surface.'

Archie knew his friend was right and his stomach was flipping out with fear but he tried to keep his voice even. 'Listen, Mr Winchester has to have a mask which means one of us must go without. I've done the Advanced Navy Diver Emergency Training so if one of us has to swim without an oxygen tank it should be me.'

Gemma and Barney exchanged worried glances, then nodded reluctantly. Adam Winchester placed a hand on Archie's shoulder, fixed him with a meaningful stare and mumbled something totally unintelligible.

'Did he say, *Your crunchy nose is a bit wet?*' Archie asked.

Barney laughed 'No. He said, *Your country owes you a big debt.* Then he said, *You will never be forgotten.*'

'Thank you, sir.' Archie swallowed hard. 'When you place the mask over your face it will fill with oxygen. Just breathe normally. I suggest you follow Agent X-ray through the hatch. Agent Zulu will be right behind you. They'll escort you to the surface.'

'You should go first,' Barney insisted.

Archie shook his head firmly. 'I don't want to distract

you. Your priority is to make sure the Prime Minister is safe.'

Gemma, Barney and Adam Winchester pulled the rubber balaclavas over their heads, slung their oxygen cylinders on their backs and adjusted their masks. Archie took his last opportunity to take some deep breaths, filling his lungs and forcing as much oxygen as possible into his bloodstream.

'Ready,' Gemma announced, giving the others a thumbs up. Barney and the PM responded with the same hand signal.

'OK, let's get out of here,' Archie said. 'This place is a wreck.'

Barney reached overhead and rotated the cross-shaped handle on the outer hatch. The latch turned slowly at first, then spun freely, withdrawing four integral locking bolts. A motor began to drive the hatch open.

Archie took one last deep breath.

Then the freezing ocean cascaded into the chamber and closed over his head.

Chapter 37

The water was like an icy mask pressing against Archie's bare face. He felt trapped and helpless – like he'd been buried in a watery coffin.

When the water was no longer gushing around his ears Archie knew the capsule was completely flooded. He watched Gemma's blurry outline swim through the hatch, then he gestured to the Prime Minister to follow. Barney went next and Archie swam after him.

Archie placed his hands on the rim of the hatch and propelled himself into the blackness above.

He looked ahead, hoping to see the pale shimmer of moonlight on the surface but his eyes were met by nothing but darkness. Such absence of light would be impossible to find even in the remotest part of the world, where stars or clouds or distant towns always reflect some sort of illumination. Only as a child, accidentally shutting himself in his mother's wardrobe, had Archie ever experienced such all consuming, terrifying blackness.

He looked round for a glimpse of his fellow agent's head-torches but they had already been swallowed by the dark. Kicking hard, he pulled the water back with his arms, following the path of the bubbles that he released through his pursed lips. The immense pressure of the sea squeezed agonisingly on his temples and his eardrums, like a tightening vice.

He took another mighty stroke. His heart was pounding. Still nothing to see but blackness.

Two more desperate strokes. The veins in his throat were throbbing and his brain was pulsating.

Everything was still black.

Maybe he'd taken on too much? Maybe the sub had sunk further than he could swim holding his breath?

His breaststroke pull was weakening and his lungs were convulsing – crying out for oxygen. He fought the instinct to open his mouth wide and gasp for air because he knew it would mean certain death. He had to keep swimming but he knew he couldn't manage more than a few more seconds.

Subversive thoughts swam into Archie's head as oxygen starvation started to take its toll on his brain.

Maybe it wouldn't be so bad to end it all here. Just take a lungful of seawater and all the agony will be over.

A movement above caught his eye and he banished the seductive appeal of surrender from his mind. After another stroke he saw a flicker of light.

Out of the darkness emerged a faint row of tiny white lights and he knew it was the head-torch belonging to one of his fellow agents, searching the depths for him.

Ignoring the screaming pain in his chest and the unbearable constriction of his throat, he kicked for all he was worth. Punching through the surface with a scream he gasped in the cool night air.

Glancing around he saw three heads bobbing in the silvery moonlight.

'Where's the Dragonfly?' he asked, his lungs heaving as he spoke.

'Over there,' Barney replied. 'Bearing zero-six-zero degrees, approximate range two hundred yards.'

Archie looked at his watch. It was ten o'clock – T minus two hours.

'Well what are you all waiting for? Last one there's a numbskull.'

Five minutes later Archie helped the Prime Minister into the plane's cockpit, watched from the back seats by Barney and Gemma.

'I'm very sorry, Prime Minister, sir,' Archie mumbled sheepishly. 'I didn't mean to call you a numbskull.'

Adam Winchester mumbled something and his good eye narrowed with amusement.

'He says he's been called worse,' Barney said. 'Usually by the Home Secretary.'

Dripping and shivering, Archie flipped open a small compartment in the cockpit's central console and took out a spare pair of glasses – his others having been washed off somewhere in the sinking submarine. He slid the canopy closed and swept his hands across the aircraft's control panels, flicking switches and pressing buttons.

Within a minute the Dragonfly's two jet engines whined into life, Archie threw the throttles forward and the plane lifted off and speared into the sky.

As the jet ripped through the night, heading for London, Gemma called Helen Highwater and gave her an update on the mission, putting her on speakerphone so the other STINKBOMB agents could hear the conversation.

When Gemma had completed her summary of recent events, Highwater responded sharply. 'When this is over I shall debrief you all on the importance of maintaining regular comms and following orders. But first of all we have to get the Prime Minister into Number Ten. Where is Yankee planning to land?'

'Right in the middle of Downing Street,' Archie replied, glancing anxiously at the plane's flight management computer. 'Our ETA is twenty-three fifty. We won't have time for secrecy.'

'That isn't no big ting,' Holden Grey chipped in. 'We'll file you as a diplomatic flight and clear any journalists from the proximate vicinity nearby.'

'We can probably substitute the constable on the door.' Highwater added, 'Use passcode six-bravo to let him know who you are. But that's as far as STINKBOMB's clearance level will get you. Once you're inside the building you're on your own. Is that understood?'

'Understood,' Archie and Gemma replied.

Barney was munching a packet of crisps. 'Copy that,' he replied, spraying the glass canopy with moist yellow globules. 'The three little pigs will flush out the wolf in sheep's clothing from the lion's den.'

'Thank you, Zulu,' Highwater sighed. 'Good luck.'

'Remember what's at stake, team,' Grey said. 'The national security of the nation.'

Gemma hung up and stared through the glass at the sea shimmering five hundred feet below. 'It's not just our nation that's in danger though,' she mumbled. 'It's all of them.'

Archie flew the Dragonfly low over the Essex countryside, echoing the gentle rise and fall of the terrain. Ripping over the twinkling lights of London, he thought about the millions of people living in the mosaic of buildings spread as far as he could see. He knew their safety depended on STINKBOMB's success in the next – he glanced at his watch – fifteen minutes.

Over the river Archie descended to a hundred feet. Reaching Big Ben he banked hard, snapping the jet on to its wingtip. Easing the power back he lowered the Dragonfly on to the ground, directly in front of the iconic Georgian house with a glossy black door.

Archie and Barney jumped out of the plane and ran over to the policeman guarding the entrance to 10 Downing Street.

314

'The sun rises in the east,' Barney announced breathlessly.

The policeman gave him an impatient frown, but then his eyes slowly widened as the realisation dawned. Fumbling in his pocket he produced a small notebook and flipped it open.

'Ah, yes, the sun rises in the east,' he muttered, then clearly recited: 'And it sets in the west.'

'Every day,' Barney replied, completing the sequence.

The policeman looked amazed. 'You're the MI6 operatives? In my fifteen years as a police off—'

'Can you open the door, please?' Archie interrupted firmly, tapping his watch. 'We're kind of in a hurry.'

With a deferential nod the PC opened the glossy black door. Archie checked his watch as he led the others into 10 Downing Street.

It was two minutes to midnight.

315

Chapter 38

In the Cabinet Room inside the Prime Minister's residence, Kurt Von Grosskopf was sitting at the head of a long wooden table. He was rather enjoying running the country – everyone doing exactly as he said, with no Klaus or Evelyn Tension bossing him around. Every one of the cabinet ministers was seated around the table alongside the most senior officers in each of the armed forces. Nobody spoke. All eyes were on the digital clock on the desk.

Kurt sat forward and leaned his elbows on the table. 'Well I think it's pretty clear the Swiss have no intention of complying with our demands,' he announced. 'Admiral Johnston, give the order to launch the first wave of missiles.'

316

The admiral glanced reluctantly at the phone in front of him, which gave him a hotline to the commander of a Vanguard submarine armed with nuclear warheads. He was stocky with short iron-grey hair. His uniform was festooned with gold braid and his chest was covered in rows of ribbon squares. His hand hovered over the receiver.

'Is there a problem, Admiral?' Kurt demanded.

'The time is twenty-three fifty-nine, Prime Minister,' the admiral replied impassively. 'There's still one minute to the deadline.'

'Ah, that's what I've always liked about you, Admiral.' Kurt smiled coldly. 'You're such a stickler for the rules. What would I do without you? OK then, hold the order. Although I can't imagine anything's going to happen in the next sixty seconds to change the course of history.'

The real Adam Winchester led the way up a flight of stairs decorated with portraits of every previous resident of Number Ten. Reaching the landing he turned right, then stopped dead. Archie, Barney and Gemma gathered behind him, eyeing the two Secret Service agents guarding the entrance to the Cabinet Room.

317

Archie stepped in front of Adam Winchester and addressed the agent whose squashed features he recognised.

'Sergeant Small,' he said as casually as he could. 'We meet again.'

'Oh no!' Ivan gasped with feigned urgency while the other agent called for back-up. 'What fantastic threat to national security have you dreamed up this time, kid? Don't tell me that a bionic man is hiding somewhere in the Cabinet Room ready to assassinate the Prime Minister?'

'No!' Barney panted emphatically. 'Actually the bionic *woman's* evil henchman is in there, wearing a rubber mask and posing as the PM so that he can steer the world into nuclear Armageddon.'

'Well why on earth didn't you say so?' Ivan laughed sarcastically. 'That's *so* much more believable.'

Gemma planted her hands on her hips indignantly. 'Listen, we wouldn't be in this mess if you hadn't given the impostor an armed escort into the heart of the government.'

'That's funny.' Suddenly Ivan's mirthless smile disappeared and he produced a snub-nosed handgun from inside his jacket. 'Now put your hands behind your heads. All of you.'

Archie's instincts told him to charge Ivan. He knew he would probably take a bullet but it might distract the bodyguards long enough for the others to get Adam Winchester inside the Cabinet Room and expose Klaus's brother as an impostor. Then he heard footsteps behind him and he instinctively knew that they were surrounded.

Archie felt someone grab his wrists and yank them behind his back. A whack to the back of his knees buckled his legs and he was forced on to the floor, his face pressed against the plush carpet.

Lying flat on his stomach he could see the other agents had also been forced to the ground. He was face to face with Adam Winchester, whose continuous cries were distorted beyond recognition by the tape over his face.

'What's he saying?' Archie asked, sensing the Prime Minister was trying to communicate with him.

'He says he'd devised a passcode for his family to use if they need to see him in an emergency,' Barney reported through squashed lips. 'It's designed to give them access to him, whatever the security situation. It might be worth a try.'

319

'Well what is it?' Gemma asked, struggling against the agent holding her down.

Adam Winchester emitted a series of desperate moans.

Interpreting the message, Archie struggled to raise his head an inch and announced, 'I've fuzzy white hair. I'm Carbon Pete!'

'Good for you,' Ivan laughed. 'Take them away.'

'That's not the code,' Barney grimaced, adding, at the top of his voice, 'I am Buzz Lightyear. I come in peace.'

The clock on the desk in the Cabinet Room read 00:00.

'Well, ladies and gentlemen,' the fake Prime Minister sneered. 'I'm sure even the admiral will agree that the deadline has now passed?'

A murmur of agreement rippled round the room.

'Make the call, Admiral.'

'Yes, Prime Minister.' The senior naval officer nodded, picked up the phone and held it to his ear. He spoke into the receiver with quiet authority. 'Yes, this is Admiral Johnston. I order you to launch strike one. Launch code alpha-seven-uniform-tango-three—'

The admiral was interrupted by the door swinging

320

open and slamming against the wall.

'STOP!' Archie yelled as he burst into the room.

'What are these children doing here, Agent Small?' Kurt snarled.

Ivan shrugged. 'They're unarmed and they gave the familial code. My orders are to let them see you.'

'Fine,' Kurt snapped. 'Well, they've seen me. Now *my* orders are to arrest them and charge them with treason.'

'Wait!' Archie protested, looking at the famous political faces around the room. Every pair of eyes was on him, everyone waiting to hear what he had to say. He jabbed a finger at the phoney Prime Minister. 'That man is not Adam Winchester!' he announced dramatically.

Bewildered silence greeted his claim.

'This is!'

Adam Winchester stepped into the room.

A series of gasps was followed by utter silence.

'An ex-MI6 Scalpel called Evelyn Tension kidnapped the Prime Minister from the Student Games earlier today. That man –' Archie jabbed a finger at Kurt – 'is one of her henchmen. His real name is Kurt Von Grosskopf and he is wearing a disguise created by a

Face-mapping-quick-drying-liquid-latex-mask-gun. Tension was deliberately steering the world to nuclear destruction to get back at Mr Winchester for revoking her licence to kill.'

As he finished speaking it occurred to Archie that the whole explanation probably sounded a little far-fetched. He compared the dishevelled Prime Minister to the polished, well-dressed impostor, and realised his argument was pretty flimsy.

With one eye bruised and swollen shut like a plum the real Prime Minister's other eye stared wildly around the room. The silver square stuck over his nose and mouth gave him a sinister air and the wetsuit was a ridiculous flourish. He looked more like a lunatic asylum escapee than a world-renowned statesman. In contrast Kurt was smart and groomed and supremely confident.

'I wonder,' Archie challenged, holding Kurt's stare. 'Had you thought Tension's plan through far enough to realise that you were supposed to die along with millions of others?'

Momentarily a shadow of uncertainty passed over Kurt's face and Archie thought he had touched a nerve.

'OK, I give in,' Kurt said.

'Sorry?' Archie asked.

'It's a fair cop,' said the impostor, the corners of his mouth twitching. 'Take me away and let this bedraggled bug-eyed idiot run the country.'

After a moment's uncertain silence someone at the far end of the table started to laugh. Realisation that their boss had indeed cracked a joke spread round the room like a wave and soon everybody was hooting with laughter at the hilarious comment.

'Silence!' Kurt roared. The laughter died immediately. 'Get these intruders out of my sight immediately.'

Archie felt someone grab his shoulder and march him roughly towards the exit. He felt utterly wretched. He had failed and soon the world would be on course for nuclear oblivion.

'I can't believe no one saw through him,' Gemma said, her jaw clenching with frustration.

Suddenly Archie's mind was racing. *What would you need to see through something?*

He remembered Holden Grey demonstrating the spiPhone and explaining the effect its X-ray camera had on certain materials. Then he thought about Evelyn Tension bragging about Klaus's innovations with the mask-gun.

'Eighty picometres!' he exclaimed.

Archie shrugged off his escort and spun round. Advancing towards Kurt he took out his spiPhone and opened its X-ray camera app.

'Prime Minister,' he called. 'Say cheese.'

Archie felt an immense force drive into his back. The camera phone flashed just as it was tossed from his grasp. He crashed to the floor, pinned down by Ivan's powerful tackle. For a moment he lay still, wondering if he'd managed to snap his target before Ivan had flattened him.

But when Archie got to his feet Kurt was smiling triumphantly at him and he deduced the camera's X-rays must have missed.

'I can see you are the sort of boy who has the courage of his convictions,' Kurt said smarmily. 'Well, after today's performance you'll be getting plenty of convictions.' Looking around the table at the cabinet he chuckled smugly.

No one laughed.

'Oh come on!' Kurt protested. 'It's a joke – he'll be getting plenty of *convictions.*'

One or two mouths opened but not with amusement. Everyone was watching the PM in absolute horror.

His lips had started to shrivel up and his whole face

324

was sagging. One eye was drooping horribly and his nose had come loose and was sliding slowly down his face. His whole head seemed to be melting – like a wax candle near an open fire. First one ear, then the other slipped, then dropped to the floor, and then his hair came away in clumps – sliding down his skull and falling to his shoulders.

Within a minute all the healthy tanned skin on his face had disintegrated, leaving a pale featureless stump with a hole where its nose should have been – like a one-eyed tortoise, in an expensive suit.

'What are you staring at?' Kurt Von Grosskopf demanded, oblivious to the transformation he'd undergone. 'Get these children out of my sight.'

Ivan relaxed his grip and Archie sprang to his feet.

'That's an order!' Kurt shrieked.

'Bad news, Von Grosskopf,' said Archie. 'You've really lost your looks.'

Realising that he'd been exposed, Kurt shoved back his chair and lunged at Archie, screaming furiously. Archie deftly spun round on one leg, swinging the other in a rising arc. His heel connected with Kurt's advancing jaw and the villain dropped to the floor like a bag of sand. Instantly two bodyguards handcuffed him and dragged him away.

'Talk about losing face,' Barney muttered, shaking his head as Archie approached.

'I know,' Gemma agreed. 'When you snapped him, his face really fell.'

'He had some people fooled.' Archie smiled. 'But the camera never lies.'

The real Adam Winchester was surrounded by cabinet colleagues. Having finally recognised their Prime Minister in spite of his battered appearance, they were desperate to offer him every sympathy for his ordeal.

Grabbing a piece of paper from the desk the PM scribbled a note and handed it to Admiral Johnston. The naval officer nodded and picked up the phone.

'This is Admiral Johnston. Cancel the launch, I repeat, cancel the launch. Stand down all missiles . . . That is correct – Prime Minister's orders.'

'We did it!' Archie exclaimed, punching the air. As he high-fived Barney and Gemma he suddenly felt his tired body throbbing with aches and pains.

With a raised finger Adam Winchester excused himself from the group and approached the STINKBOMB agents. Shaking their hands he mumbled enthusiastically for a while before turning back to the politicians.

'What did he say?' Archie asked.

'He said we did a great thing for our country today,' Barney explained. 'He also said we were a credit to the Secret Service and that we should be proud of saving millions of lives.'

Archie and Gemma shrugged humbly.

'Oh yeah,' Barney continued. 'And he said I was probably the most impressive undercover operative he's ever known.'

'Whatever,' Gemma laughed, playfully shoving Barney. 'Don't push it, Zulu.'

'Hey.' Barney held his palms upward. 'Why is that so hard to believe?'

'I'm with you, Zulu,' Archie insisted with mock sincerity. 'Even if he didn't actually say it, I'm sure he was thinking it.'

Smiling wryly, Ivan approached Archie and held his palm up. Archie high-fived him. 'Nice spinning back-kick, kid,' Ivan said. 'Where did you learn to fight like that?'

'That's classified,' Archie replied, adjusting his glasses. 'I could tell you, but then I'd have to kill you.'

As the STINKBOMB agents headed for the door, ready to fly back to HQ for their mission debrief, a corpulent figure stepped across their path. His olive skin was shiny with perspiration and his oily black hair curled up over his collar.

'Agents!' he said with an obsequious smile. 'It's so nice to finally meet you in person – I'm Hugh Figo. You can call me sir.'

Archie'd had no idea that the man who had been sitting around the cabinet table was Helen Highwater's boss. 'Pleased to meet you, sir,' he said, shaking the pudgy wet hand he was offered.

'Listen,' Figo said, lowering his voice. 'You did an excellent job today. Excellent. You were an enormous help.'

'Help?' Archie repeated.

Gemma folded her arms and dropped a hip. 'If by "help" you mean that we prevented a worldwide nuclear disaster and saved the Prime Minister from certain death then, yeah, we were a *help*.'

Hugh Figo chuckled good-naturedly. 'Let's not get carried away,' he soothed. 'I was working this thing from the inside. As the endgame approached I was

328

preparing to put my plan into action.' As he spoke his eyes darted constantly as though he was trying to keep track of a fly.

'I guess you had a code seven albatross ready to roll?' Barney asked.

'Exactly!' Figo exclaimed gratefully. 'Look, the important thing is that good triumphed over evil, no?'

'Whatever,' Gemma scoffed.

'I just have to stress that what went on in this room must never, ever be repeated to civilians.' Figo looked sternly at each child in turn until they nodded their consent. 'Don't worry though. Credit will go where credit's due. You have my word on that.'

Buttoning his jacket tightly around his large tummy, Hugh Figo turned and waddled away.

'I don't trust him,' Gemma stated.

'He was taken in by the fake PM every step of the way,' Archie sneered. 'I seriously doubt he was planning to make any kind of move.'

'I'm sure he wasn't,' Barney agreed. 'There's no such thing as a code seven albatross.'

Chapter 39

'Good morning, class,' Miss Toogood said brightly. 'I hope you all had a good weekend. As you know, some very exciting things happened on Saturday night.'

'Did Hunt get a new registration in his plane-spotter's logbook?' Newman laughed.

'Three, actually,' said Archie, squinting through his spectacles. A ripple of amusement passed round the classroom.

'I'm referring to something even more exciting than Archie's logbook.' Miss Toogood smiled kindly at Archie. 'Anybody?'

Archie raised his bandaged hand. 'Are you talking about the stand-off between Britain and Switzerland?'

'Exactly.' Miss Toogood opened her palms. 'Does

anybody know what caused the crisis?'

'Didn't Adam Winchester find out they were making nuclear bombs in their chocolate factories or something?' said Holly Jenkins.

'Yeah,' Newman agreed enthusiastically. 'So our guy said he'd blitz them, you know, nuclearly, if they didn't fess up.'

Miss Toogood nodded. 'That's about it – in a very small nutshell. Our guy – Adam Winchester, the Prime Minister – set a deadline of midnight on Saturday for the Swiss government to comply with his demands. The cabinet gathered in Ten Downing Street with some top military officers and Secret Service officials, waiting to hear from the Swiss Ambassador. At a minute to midnight there was still no word from Switzerland and we were literally teetering on the brink of nuclear war.' The class was in rapt silence. 'Then something happened that changed the course of history – and probably saved the world. Does anybody know what stopped the Prime Minister launching those missiles?'

Miss Toogood looked around the classroom at the pairs of wide eyes and open mouths.

'Barney?'

'Yes, miss?' Barney replied, his blue eyes wider than most.

Miss Toogood approached his desk. 'Do you know who saved the world?'

'It wasn't me, miss,' Barney gabbled. 'And it wasn't Archie either.'

The classroom exploded with laughter.

'Really?' Miss Toogood teased with mock disbelief. 'You didn't avert certain disaster in Ten Downing Street on Saturday night?'

'No, miss. We didn't rescue the real Prime Minister from an evil villain's lair and fly him back to Downing Street to confront the dude who was posing as Adam Winchester so that he could deliberately start a nuclear war. And Archie didn't use his X-ray camera to melt the bad guy's rubber mask so everyone could see he was a fake.'

Everyone in the class was hooting with laughter. All around the room children had fat tears rolling down their red cheeks as they gasped for breath between their hysterical peals.

'OK, Barney,' said Miss Toogood reassuringly. 'I believe you.'

Barney turned and winked at Archie.

The teacher continued. 'What happened was that the cabinet ministers spent hours rigorously inspecting the dossier on the Swiss bomb factories. At the very last minute Adam Winchester identified a detail that discredited the entire document so he called off the nuclear strike.' Winking at Barney she added, 'Although, to be honest, I much prefer Barney's story about rescuing the Prime Minister from an evil mastermind's submarine . . . OK, everyone, open your textbooks at page fifteen.'

'Where've you been?' Barney asked Archie, his mouth full of cheese sandwich. 'I thought we were going to play chess. Lunchtime's nearly over.'

Archie sat opposite Barney. Resting his elbows on the table he leaned forward. 'I've been talking to Gemma,' he whispered, glancing both ways to check they couldn't be overheard.

'Why? What's up?'

'Miss Toogood,' Archie stated.

'Oh, right.' Barney nodded knowingly, then his eyebrows dipped. 'What about her?'

'In class earlier she said she liked your story about rescuing the Prime Minister from an evil mastermind's submarine.'

'So?'

'You'd never mentioned anything about the sub.'

Barney's mouth fell open. 'So how did she know about it?'

'At first I thought she must be part of MI6.'

'Good call.'

'Gemma checked.' Archie shook his head. 'She's nothing to do with the Secret Service or any government organisation.'

Deep in thought, Barney sank his teeth into his sandwich. 'So she must have been bugging us throughout the whole op?' he concluded, spraying Archie with wet crumbs.

'That's not all.' Archie removed his glasses to wipe them and slid them back on. 'Toogood told us Moore the Bore had broken her arm so I asked Gemma to check the local hospitals.'

'And?'

'No hospitals have any record of Miss Moore being treated for a broken arm. In fact none of her friends have heard from her in over a week. Her house is empty.'

'She's missing!' Barney yelped, then lowering his voice he asked, 'Do you think Miss Toogood is involved?'

Archie nodded slowly. 'It's too much of a coincidence,' he whispered. 'I have no idea what she's up to but I think our friendly supply teacher is simply Toogood to be true . . .'

Name: # Archie Hunt

S.T.I.N.K.B.O.M.B. codename:
Agent Yankee

Age: 12

Appearance: Brown messy
hair, glasses

Hobbies: Flying, reading,
swimming

Favourite food: Pizza, milkshake

Personality: Clever, single-minded and loyal.
Becomes competitive when his ability is
challenged or doubted.

Special skills: Talented (secret)
pilot, capable of flying Dragonfly
jet aircraft in challenging
circumstances.

Most likely to say: 'I'm not
exactly one of the in-
crowd. I don't play football
and I have a slightly
nerdy obsession with
aeroplanes.'

Name: Barney Jones

S.T.I.N.K.B.O.M.B.
codename: Agent Zulu

Age: 12

Appearance: Blue eyes, blond curls, stocky (i.e. tubby) build

Hobbies: Reading (anything to do with spies), watching TV (anything to do with spies) and going to the cinema (anything to do with spies)

Favourite food: Cheeseburgers, chicken nuggets, sausages, pizza (all with chips, please), ice-cream, sponge and custard, Banoffee pie, trifle, Mars, Twix, Bounty, Snickers, Maltesers, Monster Munch

Personality: Energetic and enthusiastic. Has the potential to become overexcited in the field.

Special skills: In-depth knowledge of spy fiction (see Hobbies), which may provide on-the-money intel on Odious Masterminds' secret lairs. Must try and limit his use of spy jargon to occasions when he actually understands what he is saying.

Most likely to say: 'All units, we have a code yellow – the badger has entered the stingray's cave.'
'Are you going to finish those chips?'

Name: # Gemma Croft

S.T.I.N.K.B.O.M.B. codename:
  Agent X-ray

Age: 14

Appearance: Blue eyes, often
  rolled, straight dark hair
  with asymmetric fringe

Hobbies: Shopping, Facebooking,
    listening to music, reading
    (esp. Twilight novels)

Favourite food: Tuna salad

Personality: A sullen and often
      cynical facade masks a strong team
      ethic and motivation. Is naturally
      suspicious of strangers/newcomers,
    who will have to work hard to earn her
  respect.

Special skills: Mathematically gifted. Exceptional
  knowledge of computer technology – able to gain
  access to any website or mainframe.

Typical quotes: 'Keep your voice down,
  motormouth.'

'Whatever.'

Name: # Helen Highwater

S.T.I.N.K.B.O.M.B. codename:
IC (Initiative Commander)

Age: Claims to be 49 (official records show her to be 53)

Appearance: Brunette, angular bob. Grey, cold eyes

Interests: Theatre, Renaissance art, the symphonies of Beethoven and Brahms. (NB Although she claims to detest the insipid emptiness of pop music, colleagues report that she is often overheard singing the songs of Westlife and JLS to herself.)

Favourite food: Indonesian-French fusion

Personality: Businesslike, authoritative. Likes to win.

Special skills: Excellent leadership and management qualities. Thinks 'outside the box', as demonstrated by her suggestion to use kids as undercover agents.

Most likely to say: 'We have an E.M.U. on our hands.'
'Does anybody understand what Agent Zulu just said?'

Name: Holden Grey

S.T.I.N.K.B.O.M.B. position: Tech Branch Specialist

Age: 73

Appearance: White, neatly parted hair (although has recently started spiking it up). Thin silver moustache

Interests: Listening to the wireless, watching *Antiques Roadshow*, *Coronation Street*, *MTV Cribs*, *The Hills*.

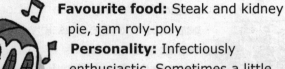

Favourite food: Steak and kidney pie, jam roly-poly

Personality: Infectiously enthusiastic. Sometimes a little overeager to connect with the young agents.

Special skills: Has a sharp mind but his knowledge of technology is twenty years behind the times. When it comes to designing gadgets his record is somewhat hit-and-miss.

Most likely to say: 'BWT, guys, the new Kaney West track is, like, so nasty? And by that I mean it's groovy.'

(Examining an iPod) 'Over a thousand songs? Surely not at the same time? How on earth do they get them in there? I can't even see the eject button.'

Name: Evelyn Tension

Age: 42 (approx)

Eyes: Green, piercing

Hair: Long, flame orange

Background: An ex-MI6 Scalpel (assassin) with a history of overstepping the limits of her mission. Thought to bear a grudge against the British Prime Minister after he revoked her licence to kill. Suspected to have her heart set on personal revenge, possibly leading to world domination.

Favourite food: Steak tartare

Personality: Vain, charming, dangerous

Special skills: Expensively educated, multilingual, with a sky-high IQ and a black belt in numerous martial arts. An exceptional master of disguise and impersonation, having perfected instantaneous spray-on-liquid-latex-face-mapping technology. All agents beware – she could be the old man in the bus queue or the schoolgirl in the park.

Name: (yet to be formally identified)

AKA: Miss Toogood

Last sighting: Classroom B3, Monday morning

Age: 37 (approx)

Eyes: Hazel

Hair: Blonde

Specialist knowledge: Biology, History, the classified missions of S.T.I.N.K.B.O.M.B. agents

Favourite food: Once seen eating a Pot Noodle in the staffroom

Personality: Kind and caring – on the surface

Background: Very little is known about Miss Toogood. She is thought to have eliminated Miss Moore (aka the Bore) and been posing as a supply teacher in order to get closer to S.T.I.N.K.B.O.M.B. agents. Could be working alone or as part of an evil syndicate.

Motivation: As yet unknown. World domination a possibility. Approach with caution – Miss Toogood is up to no good.

If there's an evil mastermind
In a secret lair
Who you gonna call?

TEAM

S.T.I.N.K. B.O.M.B.

*★Secret Team of Intrepid-Natured Kids
Battling Odious Masterminds (Basically)*

ROB STEVENS

Much to his surprise, **Archie Hunt** has been recruited into MI6's fledgling branch of teen agents. His fellow agents are **Barney** ('Are you going to finish those chips?') **Jones** and **Gemma** ('Oh, grow up!') **Croft**. Their mission? To track down the enigmatic DOCTOR DOOM, whose attempts to create the ultimate super-being must be stopped. S.T.I.N.K.B.O.M.B. meet friend and foe along the way – including the poor mutants who are the products of Doom's failed experiments. Like Finn: half-man, half-goldfish. He WANTS to lead the team to the hideout, but his three-second memory means that consistency isn't his strong point . . .

**Will they defeat the odds and save the day?
AND make it back to school by Monday morning?**

**The first EXPLOSIVE adventure in this
adrenalin-fuelled comic series!**

THE MAPMAKER'S MONSTERS

BEWARE THE BUFFALOGRE!

Rob Stevens

HERE BE MAPS! AND MONSTERS! AND MAYHEM!

As newly appointed mapmaker for Admiral Rupert Lilywhite, Hugo Bailey is about to set sail for the very edges of the known world.

But even in his wildest dreams (or should that be worst nightmares?) Hugo hadn't imagined being stranded on an island where pigs fly, mice crack jokes and bloodthirsty buffalogres try to eat you!

A rollicking new series about making maps, making friends and making some very quick escapes . . .